Claiming the Club Princess

Devil's Tide MC

B. Sobjakken

Contents

Copyright	V
Author's Note	1
Gage	4
Mikayla	14
Gage	34
Mikayla	46
Gage	66
Mikayla	76
Shaw	86
Gage	98

Shaw	114
Mikayla	124
Shaw	138
Gage	152
Mikayla	162
Gage	170
Mikayla	180
Mikayla	196
Mikayla	202
Shaw	214
Gage	224
Shaw	238
Epilogue	246

Copyright © [2024] by [Brooke Sobjakken]

All rights reserved.

No part of this publication may be reproduced, distributed, or transmitted in any form or by any means, including photocopying, recording, or other electronic or mechanical methods, without the prior written permission of the publisher, except in the case of brief quotations embodied in critical reviews and certain other noncommercial uses permitted by copyright law. For permission requests, email author@bsobjakken.com

The characters and events portrayed in this book are fictitious. Any similarity to real persons, living or dead, is coincidental and not intended by the author.

Copyediting and proofreading by Justine Luke – justinejustreads@gmail.com

Cover by @aflowersreads

Author's Note

Hello my filthy friends,

Mikayla is **not related** to Shaw or Gage.

For a full list of content warnings, please visit my website. It can be found here.

If this is your first time reading, I hope you enjoy!

If you read The Club Princess before it was removed, then know I added over 100 pages of new goodies.

xo,

GAGE

"Count it again."

Dodge piles all the money to the left, and starts moving them back to the right on the desk. I watch next to his chair with crossed arms. This isn't how I planned to spend my Friday night, stuck in a stuffy room while a middle-aged man who sweats profusely stands behind us, torturing us with his rank B.O.

The bar's manager shifts on his feet when I glance back at him, his hand fidgeting at his side. He looks nervous, not

Copyright © [2024] by [Brooke Sobjakken]

All rights reserved.

No part of this publication may be reproduced, distributed, or transmitted in any form or by any means, including photocopying, recording, or other electronic or mechanical methods, without the prior written permission of the publisher, except in the case of brief quotations embodied in critical reviews and certain other noncommercial uses permitted by copyright law. For permission requests, email author@bsobjakken.com

The characters and events portrayed in this book are fictitious. Any similarity to real persons, living or dead, is coincidental and not intended by the author.

Copyediting and proofreading by Justine Luke – justinejustreads@gmail.com

Cover by @aflowersreads

Author's Note

Hello my filthy friends,

Mikayla is **not related** to Shaw or Gage.

For a full list of content warnings, please visit my website. It can be found here.

If this is your first time reading, I hope you enjoy!

If you read The Club Princess before it was removed, then know I added over 100 pages of new goodies.

xo,

Brooke

GAGE

"Count it again."

Dodge piles all the money to the left, and starts moving them back to the right on the desk. I watch next to his chair with crossed arms. This isn't how I planned to spend my Friday night, stuck in a stuffy room while a middle-aged man who sweats profusely stands behind us, torturing us with his rank B.O.

The bar's manager shifts on his feet when I glance back at him, his hand fidgeting at his side. He looks nervous, not

in a *I'm afraid of getting caught* kind of way, but more of a *I'm afraid to be right* kind of way.

I grind my teeth, irritated at how quickly this night went to shit. "When did you first notice the difference?"

He clears his throat, pulling at his dingy t-shirt with some faded band logo. "A few months ago. It only happened once, and I chalked it up to a cash handling error. But it's happening more often."

Dodge grunts. "Testin' ya the first time. See if ya snitch."

I clap Dodge on the shoulder, agreeing with the assessment, and roll my neck side to side. "Alright. Start pulling the tapes and give me the shift schedule."

The manager nods, moving to the second desk in a hurry to gather what I asked for. I glance back at the bills Dodge is counting with ease and clench my fist. Something tells me it wasn't someone from the town stupid enough to steal from us, which leaves us with the club and all my brothers. That betrayal hits me even worse.

Pulling my phone out to update Shaw, I pause at the text on screen. "The fuck."

Viper

Just swung by. Mik got people over.

I call him, turning to face the windows overlooking the entire bar. The privacy glass is a bit extra, but when we first opened the place, it was a way to observe before cameras got better. Exhaling through my nose, I try to control the fury gathering. This night can't get any fucking worse.

"Yeah?" Viper finally answers.

"The fuck you mean, yeah? Why else would I be calling you? Who the fuck is at the house?" I snap into the phone.

Viper shuffles on the other end, moving to get a better visual from wherever he's lounging. "Uhh. It looks like a bunch of schoolmates, I think. They're drinking in the pool and stuff."

Squeezing hard enough that I hear the phone's glass start to crack, I pinch the bridge of my nose. Viper isn't the sharpest tool in the shed, but his skills at being quiet and invisible are unmatched. "How many? Where's Mik? Who she with?"

Dodge moves to my side, waving to show me that the total came up the same, and I close my eyes briefly. I don't have time to deal with Mikayla's antics, not tonight.

"About ten lingering around. Just Mik, Talia, and some guy in the hot tub," Viper says.

My shoulders stiffen, and a different anger makes my voice cold. "Mik in the hot tub with some guy?"

"I mean, he's in the hot tub. Yeah." His vague answer tells me more than he wanted it to. Viper spends a lot of time watching Mikayla, almost like a personal bodyguard, and I know he's grown protective. It's why I trust him more than most.

I catch Dodge's raised eyebrow, and the smirk starting to curl on his lips. With clenched teeth, I hang up on Viper without another word and turn back to the manager. The man is shaking as he stands, waiting for my next command.

"Go ahead. I'll be right behind ya with the stuff," Dodge offers with a chuckle. We're all used to her antics by now, but only Shaw and I are the ones unamused.

Pulling my keys out of my pocket, I shake my head. "I'm gonna spank her ass."

His laughter booms in the small room as I head towards the door. "That sounds more like a punishment for ya," he taunts as I head down the stairs, and I roll my eyes at the comment.

Most of the bar patrons move out of my way as I head to the exit. Though our businesses bring a lot of money into this town, most of the judgmental pricks look down at us. Our money is good enough to take, but not enough for them to treat us with decency because we like tattoos and loud bikes.

I let out a loud whistle and quick jerk of my head to the door to signal a few of my men to follow me out.

"Gage, my man! Come take a shot!" Jack hollers from the counter.

I barely spare him a glance, even on a night I'm not in a foul mood Jack isn't my first choice to hang out with. The man uses everyone around him, particularly pussy, and isn't discreet about it. He was only initiated because of who he's related to.

Then I pause when I remember he's supposed to be in the yard with some prospects.

Stomping back into the bar, I move to stand next to Jack. "The fuck you doing here?"

His eyebrows knit together as he blinks at me, his eyes red in a drunken haze. "What?"

I grab him by his cut, pulling him out the door as he protests with loud shouts. He tries to swat at my hold, so I let go, and he falls onto his ass in the dirty parking lot.

Dodge comes flying out the door next, staring down at Jack with an impatient stare. He more than likely watched the confrontation through the windows and knew what would come next.

"You got him?" I ask Dodge. If I stay to deal with the drunk dumbass, my knuckles might end up swollen and too damaged to ride.

He nods, twisting at his beard before he sighs. "I got 'em."

When I walk away, a prospect scrambles away from where he was watching over our parked bikes, his eyes downcast. His body is tense as if waiting for some ridicule as well.

I pause before him, and I can hear his swallow. "Did Jack take y'all to the yard tonight?"

He shakes his head.

"You have my number?"

When he shakes his head again, I sigh and pull out my phone. "Call yourself. I want updates on his movements at all times, you understand? And if I find out you're covering for him, your ass is out."

The prospect agrees with a quick nod and hands back my phone. I'm sick of Jack getting away with being a freeloader simply because he's blood to Bear and Dodge.

It's time to put him back in his place if he's slacking off on his duties.

Climbing onto my bike, my body relaxes with the feel of the beast under me. This is why I do it all; every ride is worth it. The freedom of the road under my wheels and the brothers who ride next to me. I take off towards the house I rarely spend time at. When I heard dad bought it, I couldn't contain my scowl. Then he explained he didn't want Mikayla coming and going to the clubhouse as she wanted, and it all made sense. Though most nights we spend at the clubhouse, some days I still drag myself home to check on my pain in the ass sister.

Mikayla

Settling down on his lap, I lick off the salt I just sprinkled on his neck. I swallow the shot of tequila as Sean tilts his head back, his fingers digging into my hips. He thrusts up into me, his hard dick pressing against my pussy. It isn't anything impressive from what I can feel between our swimsuits. I just have to hold onto the hope he knows how to use whatever he's working with.

I shake my head and withhold the grimace as the bitter alcohol slides down my throat. I don't understand why anyone enjoys drinking; it all tastes horrible. But it's my

18th birthday, and I need to forget that the two most important people in my life forgot about me.

"Another one, bitch?" my best friend Talia asks, holding up the bottle of Patrón.

Sean grabs it from her, takes the shot glass from my hand, and sets both on the wooden bench near the hot tub's side.

"Lean back," he instructs, pouring salt between my breasts.

Smirking, I do what he asks as his hot tongue licks the wet skin, and he downs his own shot. He smacks his tongue on the roof of his mouth with a grimace and hands Talia back the bottle. "God, it's nasty."

"But I made it taste better, right?"

He smiles, his heated eyes flashing. "Of course, babe."

Talia laughs, splashing some water toward us. "Don't go getting any romantic notions. This one doesn't get tied down."

I flip her off and wrap my arms around Sean's neck. "Shove off, bitch. He knows the score."

Sean squeezes my waist, pulling me further into him. "You still joining your father's club?"

I shrug, glancing away from him. People litter my backyard for the unplanned party Talia threw together at the last minute. It's impressive that so many showed up, but I know most are looking for an "in" with my dad or brother. "I doubt they'll let me."

"Well, honestly, if it was my sister, I wouldn't want to watch her get fucked seven ways to Sunday, either," Sean says snidely.

Talia snorts, drinking straight from the glass bottle again. Her movements are getting a bit more sluggish.

I frown, wondering why she's drinking so heavily. I turn back to Sean and roll my eyes. "It's not like that. People aren't just fucking wherever and whenever they want. Most of the men have jobs during the day, ya know? It's mostly just knowing you'll have a warm body next to you when you come home."

"Yeah, but most of the men work for your dad, right? So it's not *really* a job." He laughs, and I untangle myself from him.

"It is. My father owns multiple businesses. The rumor mill runs wild, but this isn't some TV drama. He's not a criminal. The Devil's Tide just gives the men a sense of brotherhood, of belonging."

Sean reaches to pull me back, and I scoot away, no longer interested in hooking up with someone who thinks so poorly of my family. "Come on, babe. I didn't mean anything by it."

"I—"

The music cuts off, and quiet murmurs sweep across the yard. My head swivels, and a shiver of excitement runs through me when I see the thunderous scowl of my brother at the gate. Standing in his cut, with his tattooed arms folded across his chest and his sharp jaw lined with stubble, his threatening aura has always caused an inappropriate response from me since I was a teenager.

It's childish, but I only get his or my father's attention when I'm doing something I shouldn't. My mother fucked off when I was little, and neither was prepared to handle a little girl so young. It probably didn't help my daddy issues that my stepfather is just as hot as Gage. Shaw is the definition of a silver fox, his dark gray hair peppered with white was buzzed short, but his beard long enough to tug on had the same coloring. He didn't have as many tattoos as Gage, but they had similar muscular builds. When they stood next to one another, it's more than obvious they were related.

"You fuckers have one minute to get the fuck out of my house." My brother snarls, his gaze locking on me and then sliding to Sean with an even more murderous glare.

"Oh shit!" Talia squeals with a giggle. She struggles to stand, leaning heavily on the side.

I nod at Sean. "Grab her and take her home, will you?"

He pauses, looking between us with uncertainty.

Smiling, I fold my arms across my chest. "You don't want to be near me when my brother catches up."

Sean's eyes track to something behind me, and he scrambles to get out of the water, pulling Talia up. He waves bye as he walks the long way around the pool toward the back gate. I face my brother, who is storming towards me, pushing any bystanders out of the way.

"What are you doing, Mik?"

I climb out of the hot tub, fixing the straps of my white bikini as I move to stand before him with a raised brow. "Enjoying myself. Is that a crime?"

"Dad doesn't like randoms in the house. You know that." His eyes burn a path down my body. Gage swallows visibly and fixes his attention back on my face.

"And?" I say dryly.

His gaze sharpens, watching me for a moment. "What's got your panties in a twist?"

My throat burns as I try to hold back the tears stinging my eyes. We stare at each other before I step back, wanting to get away from him. I can see a few of his crew loitering around near the house.

"Do you really not know what today is?" I can't keep the hurt out of my voice.

His brows scrunch in confusion, and he pulls out his phone, checking the date. I watch his face collapse in horror, and he turns back to me. "Mik–"

I laugh, throwing up a hand. "Fuck you both. So what if Dad cares that I threw a party? Tell him I don't give a fuck, and he can shove it up his ass."

I move around him to make a dramatic exit, but Gage grabs me around the elbow, spinning me back toward him. I don't waste the opportunity, and I punch him in the face.

"Fuck!" I cry out, shaking out my aching hand as Gage rubs at his jaw. He grabs my wrist, checking my already reddening knuckles with a scowl.

"Why would you do that?" he asks.

I shrug, hissing with pain as he presses down. "Because you deserve it."

A few men behind us snicker, and Gage glares them into silence. He rubs at my hand for a few more seconds before pulling me into his chest, wrapping his arms around me.

"I'm sorry," he whispers into my hair. His smell of leather, oil, and crisp pine is overwhelming but settles something inside me. It reminds me of home.

Sighing, I hug him back. "I don't forgive you."

His body shakes as he chuckles, squeezing me tighter. His hands rest on the small of my back as he drags one up to cup the back of my neck. Tilting my head back, he looks down at me as his green eyes sparkle with mischief.

"How can I make it up to you, Princess?"

My insides twist with the endearment. I've been called it my entire life; it's a thing of honor among the men.

But it turned nasty and condescending outside the club. It feels like something else entirely when it falls from my brother's lips.

"Nothing, it's too late. The day is over." I push at his chest and step away. "I bet Dad won't even remember without you telling him."

Gage grimaces. "The club–"

I snort. "Yeah, I know, okay? The club always comes first. I get it. But... I just wanted one day."

His body slumps, and I know I'm hurting him, but I bet it's only a fraction of what I feel. "You could have reminded us."

"Right... because that's not pathetically desperate."

Gage groans. "Mikayla. We love you, but we're busy. We would never intentionally forget about your birthday."

Rolling my eyes, I grab a towel and wrap it around myself. "Duh. That's how forgetting works, dumbass."

I don't wait for a response, and I turn and walk back to the house, ignoring the club members watching me.

"Princess!" Dodge calls, setting down the beer he grabbed from who knows where. I look at him and give him a small smile. He's one of my favorites and also one of my brother's best friends.

"Dodge." I smile. He steps closer, pulling something out of his back pocket and handing the white envelope to me.

"Ain't much, but the girls always goin' on about 'em. Happy birthday, kid."

My chin quivers as tears gather, blurring my vision. Clearing my throat, I hold it close to my chest. "Thanks, Dodge."

He frowns, looking over my face. "It ain't anythin' special. No need for the waterworks."

I can feel the heat of Gage pressing into my back. "So far, it's my only present today. It's special to me."

Dodge glances over my shoulder warily. He nods, grabbing a beer from some random guy lingering and stepping away. We both know Lacy, the head bitch in charge of all the clubwhores, remembered my birthday and got me a present. Either way, it was nice to be thought of.

Gage growls low, moving to grab it from my hands, but I scurry away from him as he follows.

"What is that? What did he get you?"

Walking into the kitchen, I throw the towel on the counter and turn to face him. "I didn't exactly have time to open it!"

"Then hand it over." Gage steps closer, his eyes clouding with fury and something unmistakably darker.

I hold the envelope closer. "No, it's mine." I sound like a child, but it is mine. And I want it, no matter how small it is. Somebody thought about me on my birthday, and I want to savor it.

"Mik, I swear. Something serious is going down. It's why we dropped the ball. I'm sorry," Gage runs a hand through his dark hair, pushing it off his forehead. I love it when he keeps it longer.

I frown. "What happened?"

He stares at me, his lips thinning. I wait momentarily before huffing out a humorless laugh and shaking my head. "Of course. You won't even share why."

"You know—"

I take off to my bedroom, not wanting to hear his excuses anymore. I hear the scuffing of his boots against the tile as he hurries to follow me.

"Mikayla!" he growls. The low, scathing tone sends a sliver of fear coursing through me.

I sneak a glance as I run up the stairs, gripping the railing to propel me forward. When I see he's practically on my ass, I screech and miss the last steps, tumbling to the hallway floor leading to the bedrooms.

His hands grip my waist, flipping me over and onto my back as his body crashes over me. Snatching the envelope from my hand, he tosses it over his shoulder and gathers my wrists, slamming them on the floor.

"Why are you acting like this?!" Gage grits out through his teeth. His nostrils flare, his eyes dilate with the adrenaline of the chase.

I try to buck him off, but he just uses the movement to press his knee between my legs. He moves his body further between them, settling his hips and pushing my thighs open.

"Get off! I just want to be left alone like I always am." I spit at him.

His face softens. "I said sorry, Mik."

"Okay? And I don't forgive you. I don't have to just because you apologized."

Gage squeezes my wrists, his anger coming back. "Fine. Then what the fuck was tonight? You just throwing a party? Inviting strangers into our home."

I snort. "*Our* home, sure. What does it matter who I invite?"

"And that fucking loser who had his hands and tongue all over you. What was your plan for that? Just gonna give your virginity away to scum like him?"

It takes a moment for his words to process, and I can't stop the grin that stretches across my face. "Who says I'm still a virgin?"

Gage flinches, his gaze roaming over my face, looking for a lie. "What the fuck..."

I arch an eyebrow. "Was I supposed to save it for something? Someone? Use me as a bargaining chip to forge an alliance with another club?" I'm taunting him now. They would never do that to me, nor would they need to. The closest club is almost another state over. We mostly only get nomads rolling through.

He lets go, rolling off and sitting next to me. I slowly get up, resting my head on my raised knees.

"We would never do that, Mik." His voice is strained, and I close my eyes to avoid the hurt I'm sure is shining in his.

"I know."

He sighs, moving closer, and his arm wraps around my shoulder. "How can we make this up to you?"

My stomach is restless as I take a deep breath to ask for what I want. I look at him, biting my lip. "I want to join the club."

His eyebrows furrow. "We don't have—"

"As a club whore."

"Fuck no!" Gage furiously snaps out, his eyes narrowing to slits.

Pushing him away from me, I stand up. "Then fuck off. I'm joining the club, or I'm leaving and never coming back."

He stands with me, stepping into my space till he backs me against the wall. I swallow down my unease at the look on his face.

"Do not threaten me, Mikayla."

His palm covers my mouth before I can reply. His hard body presses into mine as he leans into my ear. "I'm going to give you the night to cool the fuck down, but you're not leaving, and you'll become a club whore over my dead fucking body."

I glare at him as his hand squeezes my cheeks in warning before letting go.

"Don't even think about trying to sneak out or sneak others in. I'll have brothers watching. I'll see you in the morning."

His gaze drags down my barely covered body again, the white bikini glowing against my tan skin, before stomping down the stairs.

GAGE

I slam through the door, not bothering to glance at the curious gazes of the men spread throughout the clubhouse. The main room has various couches along the wall and two large pool tables in the middle. A bar spans across the back, which Lacy pretty much claimed as her own.

Climbing the stairs to the second floor, I ignore the open doors and explicit activities happening for everyone to see and join if they want. When I reach the end of the hallway, I don't knock as I open my father's office.

He looks up from the paperwork sprawled on the desk with a frown, setting his glasses on the scattered mess. "Boy, who do you think you are opening my door like that?"

In the past he instilled a knocking only policy, mainly so he wouldn't get caught with his pants down. I've always ignored it, much to his displeasure. Dropping on the couch, I rub my hands down my face with a long groan. Dealing with Mikayla is more draining than a full-day ride. "She's fucking crazy."

He chuckles as I glance up at him. Crossing his arms, he leans back onto the chair. "Mik has always been a handful."

I grimace. "We forgot her birthday."

His boots drop back onto the floor as he checks his phone. "Fuck!"

"Yeah, she isn't happy." I nod, dragging my tongue along the back of my teeth, not wanting to admit the other part.

My father runs a hand through his peppered hair with a sigh. "She's going to punish us for weeks. Fuck, I don't have time to cater to her tantrum."

My knee bounces, and I stare at him till he looks back at me.

"What?"

"She proposed something."

He scowls. "What do you mean she proposed something?"

Swallowing down a grimace, I look at the floor. "She wants to join…. as a clubwhore."

"Absolutely not!" he roars, slamming a fist on the desk. I glance at the fury spanning across his face. My father is gone, and President Shaw is in his place.

I hold up my hands. "I told her the same, but she threatened to leave town since she's eighteen."

He growls, rubbing at his beard. "And where the fuck's she gonna go? With what money?"

"I didn't entertain the idea," I say with a shrug. "But she doesn't bluff, we know that."

"Mikayla isn't going to become a fucking whore. Nothing wrong with our ladies, but Mikayla isn't in a situation where this is a better life than the streets."

Nodding, I lean back on the cushions, resting my foot on my knee. "Dad, I know. I'm just saying she doesn't make idle threats."

A chuckle falls from his lips, and President Shaw fades away as the softness of my father's features returns. "What are we going to do?"

I think about the feel of her against my body, and my cock twitches. When Mikayla was sixteen, I was quickly reminded that she wasn't my blood sister, and she had grown up to be a fucking wet dream. On her birthday, she had drunkenly climbed into my lap and kissed me, saying she had the biggest crush on me. I had never gotten harder than when I could feel her soft curves after she had fallen into me. The look on her face when I pushed her away and told her I didn't feel the same still haunts me. We've avoided each other ever since.

My father is no better either, too caught up with the club's businesses to realize weeks have passed since the last time he checked on Mikayla. I know she deserves better than the two of us, but we were all that was left when her crack addict mother skipped town and left a five-year-old unattended.

"What if... we pretend to vote her in?"

My father frowns. "How would we pretend that? She's aware of the process. She has to be tried by members of the council and approved."

I lick my lips, my heart pounding as I watch his face. "We're two members of the council."

He blinks before his eyes harden, and his skin flushes red. "What the fuck are you suggesting exactly?"

"I'll fuck her, and you watch. That's two. I'll claim her as my old lady," I stammer out quickly as he stands, storming towards me. I'm barely on my feet when his hand wraps around my throat, and my back slams into the wall.

"She's your fucking sister."

I cough, swinging at his side to let me go. Shaw grunts when my knuckles collide, but he doesn't release his hold. "Not... my real... sister," I sputter out.

He drops me, pushing my chest so I fall back into the wall again. "We've raised her since she was a little girl. This isn't happening. No!"

I laugh humorlessly. "Be fucking real. We've barely spent time with her over the years. I know you saw the photo on Jack's phone from her sweet sixteen. I beat his ass for having it. She's not a little girl, and you barely even acknowledge her as your daughter."

"The club would never accept it." He tries again.

Smirking, I rub at my neck. "You're the fucking president and a fucking good one at that."

"Because they believe in me. They trust me, and I earned their loyalty. This could tarnish more than our reputation, son."

The noises of the men downstairs float through the closed door as we sit in silence. It shouldn't matter who I want to claim as my old lady. Mikayla and I aren't related, and we've never been a happy-go-lucky family.

I walk over to his desk as he follows me back to his chair. "Find anything?"

"Yeah, we're getting closer to narrowing it down."

"How much has the fucker stolen now?" I ask, clenching my teeth at the betrayal coursing through me. It hurts differently when someone you thought you could trust with your life might be the first to stab you in the back.

"Almost half a million over the past two years. He's clever, I'll give him that." My father sighs, moving the paperwork into neat piles. The dark circles under his eyes make his features gaunt, showing his age and exhaustion.

We were getting ready to start changing some of the businesses into my name when we saw the discrepancies in the books. He doesn't plan to step down as president anytime soon, but it is better to be prepared beforehand than scrambling after the fact.

After everything my father has done for this club, the fact that one of the brothers is willing to steal from him makes me angry enough to kill someone. And I know no matter how angry I am, the hurt my father feels is twice that amount.

"Have you thought about bringing this to the council?" I ask.

He grunts. "How am I supposed to trust any of them?"

"Cowen, Dodge, and Bear. They've been with us for our entire lives, and we would all kill for each other. I trust them."

My father's jaw tics. "I thought I could trust all of them."

"I don't think it's any of the council. They helped you found this club, they wouldn't betray us. But a brother we brought on from the word of another. He wouldn't put you on a pedestal like we all do."

He shakes his head, raising his eyebrow. "No one puts me on a pedestal, boy."

Shrugging, I sit on the edge of his desk. "A lot of those men were headed for a long road of drugs after you guys got out of the service. Their gratitude is obvious every day. Dodge and I used to share the same crib when you and Bear didn't have much money and our moms fucked off."

His shoulders slump, and he rubs a tired hand down his face. "I've been thinking of asking Cowen. He's better at this computer bullshit than me."

"Then that's what we'll do." I nod. "Now, back to Mikayla. If I claim her as an old lady, it will protect her if this goes south with whoever is betraying the club."

My father sits up. "Does she even want to be your old lady? Does she even see you like that?"

"What if I can prove it to you? Would that help you bring it up to the council?" I lick my lips and arrange my hardening cock in my jeans.

He scowls. "Prove what?"

"That she doesn't think of me as a brother. Like I said, we're two members of the council. She knows if she joins as a whore, any members can fuck her."

"And I'm sure she excluded us from that list." He glares at me.

I smirk. "How sure are you? Because I can bring her tonight, and if she says no, that's the end. I think you're scared of her *not* saying no."

"You're ready to put that to the test now? This can't wait till after we find the rat."

I swallow, my stomach tightening. "We're losing her. I can feel it."

He slams his palm on the wood of his desk. "Fuck. You'll do it either way. Bring her in then."

Me

Get dressed, Princess. Your birthday wish has been granted.

Mikayla

Shaking out my nerves, I knock on the door of my father's office. The men downstairs are silent as I walk up the stairs, unfamiliar with the sight of me at the clubhouse so late. Some part of me wonders if they know what will happen. I also wonder which members of the council they'll choose. I know my father would never choose Bear because of how close they are and how close his son, Dodge, is to Gage.

My brother opens the door with a taunting smirk, waving me forward, and quietly shuts it behind me as I walk into the room. My father sits behind the desk with a grim expression. He clearly is not happy about my request, so I give him my back and face Gage.

"Strip."

I tense, confused and unsure if he's joking. "R-right now?"

Gage nods, his face stoic. "You know the rules. We're a part of the council, are we not?"

My heart skips a beat, excitement swirling in my belly. I'm sure they are trying to deter me, but they will be surprised to know this won't stop me. I have had fantasies about Gage since I was old enough to know what sex was. An odd thrill runs straight to my pussy when I think about my father and the way he plans to use me tonight if they follow through and this isn't some cruel prank.

I grip the hem of my white sundress near my thighs, pull it over my head, and drop it on the floor. It leaves me in my pale blue lace bra and panties. Gage's eyes roam over my body, and his chest starts rising and falling faster.

"Everything." His voice is hoarse. Reaching back, I unclip my bra, slide the straps off my shoulders, and let it fall to the ground. Hooking my fingers into my waistband, I shimmy out of my panties, bending slightly to push them down. There's a small, sharp inhale behind me.

Standing up straight, I stare at Gage, who watches me back. His throat bobs as he swallows.

"Show me."

The deep voice from behind me makes my nipples harden more, and heat gathers in my tummy.

Gage stalks forward till he's right in front of me. His fingers brush the underside of my breasts, and goosebumps pebble along the skin. His hand skims down my waist till he grips it and turns me to face our father. He pushes me to walk until we're standing at his desk.

My father's eyes are locked on the rosy pink tips of my breasts. His tongue peeks out to rub along his bottom lip. He glances behind me at Gage and nods. "Continue."

A rough hand wraps around the nape of my neck and pushes me down, and I catch myself with my palms flat on the desk. A foot kicks my legs apart, and there's more pressure to arch my back as my hips are pulled away from the desk.

Fingertips graze my pussy, teasing along my folds. It clenches at the emptiness.

"How does it look?" my father asks. I glance up at him. His hand is rubbing against the large bulge in his pants, his gaze locking onto mine.

"Pretty *princess* pink," Gage answers.

"And how does it taste?"

There's a rustle of movement before a hot tongue licks at my entrance and then down my center to my clit. I gasp, my eyes widening.

"Like the nectar of gods," Gage mumbles against my pussy.

My father hums, unzipping his jeans and pulling his hard cock out, stroking it. I can only see half of it, but I inhale at the size. No wonder the women at the club are always begging to fuck him. It's thick, long, and the large red crown has a ridge around it that you know will drag along your walls.

Gage sucks at my clit, and my body jerks with a yelp, not used to the sensation.

"How does it feel?" my father asks.

Gage's tongue pulls away, and I try to relax for the preparation for his fingers when I hear another zipper being undone. My stomach drops, and my hands curl into fists.

Hot, hard flesh rubs along my wet center. I desperately want to see it, touch it, feel it. Gage seems to have inherited his size from his father. My legs tremble with anticipation of my brother fucking me.

"I don't know if her little pussy can handle it. I might just wreck her cunt," Gage taunts.

My father grips his cock tighter, stroking around his head, and nods. "That's what she wants, right?"

"Right," he answers before pushing into me with a harsh thrust. My mouth falls open in a silent scream as my walls ache and flutter to stretch to his size.

Fingers dig into my hips, squeezing hard.

"Oh *fuck*. She's so fucking tight." Gage groans. He rocks gently, pulling a few inches out and pushing back in repeatedly. I pant, moaning when I feel the press of his pelvis against my ass cheeks. He's inside me. My brother's cock is buried in my pussy. It's big, hot, and throbbing as we stay locked like that for a few seconds.

"You feel so good. Fuck your little sister's pussy," I beg.

"Jesus," Gage grunts, his dick twitching. He pulls out and slams back in. The movements cause me to lose my hold, and we fall. The desk digs into my hips. Gage doesn't miss a stroke as he pounds into me.

"Look at me, baby girl," my father coaxes, and I lift my head. He's standing before me. His hard cock is jutting out, his hand still wrapped around it. "Open your mouth and suck your daddy's cock."

My pussy clenches, and Gage groans.

"Fuck, she liked that."

"Let her catch her breath," my father demands, and Gage pauses his thrusting, keeping himself notched as far as he can inside me.

My father steps forward, thighs pressing against the desk. The smooth skin of his head brushes against my lips, and I lick at it. Opening my mouth wider, I suckle the tip of his dick, and he guides it in. One of his hands rests on my cheek, fingers curling under my jaw and in my hair as I suck on his cock.

Gage lifts us, pushing my upper body onto the desk and angling my ass up. It slides our father's cock further into my mouth, and I groan at the pressure on my jaw. I'm not like a master of blowjobs, but my father's dick is so beautiful. It isn't hard to love it.

His other hand lets go of his shaft, pushing my hair off my shoulder and neck, wrapping it up in a twisted ponytail.

"Our little princess wants to be our whore. Let's make sure she knows what that entails." My father growls, staring down at me as I blink up at him.

Gage pulls out and slams back into me while my father thrusts almost his entire cock down my throat. His hands tighten around my head and are unrelenting as I try to pull back when I gag. My eyes water as Gage sets a punishing pace behind me. My pussy is already aching from the abuse. I can't breathe as my father holds me in place for a few more seconds before pulling out of my mouth as I cough and splutter.

"You think you can handle our cocks, little girl?"

I nod, letting the tears stream down my face. "I'll learn to. Please, Daddy."

"Fuck." Gage groans, picking up the pace as his cock swells. "Are you on birth control, Mikayla?"

"No," I croak. His fingers tighten, and he thrusts harder and deeper into me.

"Do it," my father says. "Come inside her pussy. Make her ours." He lets go of me and steps back.

I gasp, and Gage lets out a gargled moan as the tip of his cock presses against my cervix and floods my pussy with heat. I clench as I feel the unfamiliar sensation of my walls being drenched with cum.

"Oh my god!" I cry out as Gage throbs with each pulse of his cock spraying his seed inside me.

My forehead drops to rest against the wood as we catch our breath. I didn't come, but it was still hot, and I can't wait to feel it again. Gage pulls out, his fingers replacing his cock as he pushes his cum back inside me.

"Come ride your daddy's cock, Princess," my father calls, and I turn to see him sitting on the couch, pants pushed to his ankles.

Gage helps me up and walks me over to the couch. I straddle my father's lap, my leaking pussy resting against the hard cock on his thigh. My father wraps a hand around my throat, tilting my head to face him.

"You enjoy your brother's cock?"

I lick my lips and nod.

"Yeah? And now, are you going to be a good girl and come all over your daddy's lap?" he asks, his heated eyes roaming all over my body.

I nod again and reach between us. I put the head of his cock at my entrance, settling down on the tip. His other hand pinches at my nipple, twisting it. I gasp and sink down. He lets go of my throat to cup my other breast, leaning forward to pull the taut bud into his mouth. My fingers curl into his salt-and-pepper hair as I continue to push down onto the monster that is his cock. It stretches me so full that I swear it will burst through my belly. Even with the extra lubricant of Gage's cum, he's pushing my limits.

"That's it." He coos around the mouthful of my breast. "Nice and slow."

"I don't know if it will fit," I say pitifully, glancing at Gage, who is watching us with curious eyes.

My father's hands glide to my hips, fingers flexing as he thrusts gently. "It will, baby. You're taking it so well already."

The ache between my legs burns. I stop and shake my head. "I can't, Daddy."

He pulls my face to him, kissing me softly. His tongue coaxes its way in and devours my mouth. His thumb drags down to my clit, circling it. When my pussy clenches around his cock, it's borderline painful. There's no room for the squeeze. I'm already stretched full.

My father pulls away, and his hands slide to my waist to push me back. When I start to lean, he grabs my thigh, lifting it over his lap and turning me around. I grasp onto his knees, facing away from him now. He's barely even moved out of me.

"Get your sister ready to take all of me," he commands, and Gage walks over with a smirk, dropping to his knees in front of me.

"Gage?"

"Shh. Relax, Princess. We got you," he says.

My father's hands grip my chest, fingers squeezing at my breasts, and he pulls me till my back is flush with his front.

Gage rubs at my clit, my pussy clenching on the top of the cock still buried inside. "Just got to get her a little wetter, hmm?"

He leans forward, sucking the swollen bundles of nerves. I jerk forward, but my father clamps down on my hips to hold me in place.

"No, no. Too much!" I cry out.

Gage chuckles, swirling his tongue right above where his father is slowly starting to slide further into me. "There we go, baby girl. Stretch around that cock."

"Oh my god." I lean back, and my father's fingers drift up to pinch and twist at my nipples. I gush at the attention from all fronts, his hard length pushing in more.

My pussy is being stretched to a painful limit, and I rock my hips towards Gage's face. When I finally feel my ass cheeks meeting my father's pelvis, I let out a shaky sigh. "Is that all?"

Gage nods. "Yeah, Princess. You did so good taking all of him. Look at how red and swollen you are from taking this monster."

Our father grunts behind me. His hands guide my hips to lift halfway before he pulls me back down. I gasp at the motion of his cock dragging along my walls.

"Tell him," Gage encourages.

I frown. "Tell him what?"

"Tell him you want him to lay you out and pound into your tight little pussy until he fills it with his cum."

I flutter around my father's cock at the image Gage painted.

"Please," I whimper.

My brother smirks, looking behind me. "Please what, Princess? Use your words."

I'm pushed forward, my arms wrapping around Gage's neck as my father's hands slide under my knees. He pulls me up before dropping me back on his cock as he thrusts up.

"*Ahhhhh!*" I scream. My vision goes spotty from his large girth. The stretch is painful and pleasurable at the same time.

Gage swipes the hair off my forehead, pressing soft kisses along my face. "You have to be quieter, Princess."

I whimper as my father continues to pummel my pussy, my nails clawing into Gage's neck. "*Oh my god. Oh my god.*"

"Fuck, she's strangling my cock." My father groans.

Gage laughs. "It's been a minute since you've broken in such young cunt, hasn't it?"

I feel him twitching inside me, and I gasp, dropping my head onto my brother's shoulder. His hands drift between us, rubbing at my clit.

My head snaps back to stare at him. "No, no." It's too much, I can't possibly come again.

My father grunts as I clamp down on his cock, trying to move in and out of me. "Make her come. You want my cum, baby? Milk it from me."

I try to shake my head, but Gage devours my mouth with his, pushing his tongue in. His fingers play at my clit, making my body tremble as it starts to tighten from my impending orgasm. My father picks up his pace with deep thrusts.

I feel him start to swell inside me, his hands tightening on my legs with bruising strength as I feel the first pulse of his cum spilling. Gage bites at my bottom lip, pinches my sensitive clit with his fingers, and I jerk. The waves of pleasure crash through me as I come, my father cursing behind me as he pushes his cum deeper with slow strokes.

Gage pulls away, leaving me panting with loud heaves. His gaze drops to where my father's cock slips out of me, leaving my sore pussy empty and aching.

"Look at you. So full of cum you're painting the floor with it," Gage whispers tenderly. He kisses me again before grabbing me under my arms and pulling me into his chest. My father lets go, and I cling to Gage.

Looking behind me, I see him tuck his cock back into his pants as he walks to the desk and grabs some paper towels.

My father pauses when he notices me watching, and I can see the swallow of his throat.

"You okay?"

I nod, nuzzling my face into Gage's neck.

My father sighs and kneels down to our level. "Happy Birthday, Mikayla."

Smiling, I close my eyes as Gage holds onto me, falling asleep in the comfort of his arms.

GAGE

I smack the vibrating phone off the nightstand with a groan. The barely visible light peeking through the curtains tells me it's still early morning. I've probably only gotten a few hours of sleep after bringing Mikayla home from the clubhouse.

Sitting up, I rub a hand down my tired face and lean over the side of the bed to scoop up my phone. I squint at the bright screen and curse when I read the string of texts.

Mikayla shifts in bed, pulling the sheets closer to her as she burrows into her pillow. My chest already aches at the thought of leaving her side. I run my finger over her bare shoulder, in awe that we got to claim her last night. I'm still shocked I got my father to agree to the arrangement. I'd been resigned to the fact she would never be mine.

Climbing out of bed, I move over to her side and brush the hair off her face. She's always slept like the dead. I can't remember how many nights I snuck in and just laid in bed with her, controlling the urge to touch her. Not being sure she felt the same was the only thing that stopped me.

When the phone in my hand vibrates again, I debate crushing it before I turn and leave her in bed to grab a quick shower. She's still asleep when I come out of the bathroom, and I watch her the entire time I dress and grab my cut with a sigh. I wish she was awake so I could grab a kiss goodbye.

I jog down the stairs and nod at Viper in the kitchen. I'm used to him always being around and awake. I'm not sure when he sleeps to be honest.

"You get a message to head to church?" I ask, grabbing an energy drink from the fridge and gulping it down.

He shakes his head, eating his bagel while staring at me with his large eyes. People who aren't used to it always get freaked out by that stare. The brother's joke that he got his name because he doesn't blink enough, reminding them of a snake.

"You good then if I leave you here with Mik? I'll be back as soon as I can."

Viper nods, snatching a napkin and wiping his mouth. "Can I change the alarm code? And check out the camera systems."

I frown. "Why?"

"Vibes," he says blankly.

My eyebrows raise and I scoff out a small laugh. "Whatever. Just make sure to text me and Cowen the code."

· ♥ · ♥ · ♥ · ♥ · ♥ ·

The prospect is waiting by the far end of the bar, hidden by the shadows of the liquor display. I nod at the bartender, grab us both a beer, and head over.

His eyes widen when I offer him the drink, and I smirk. "It's not a test. You can take it."

He grabs it hesitantly and gulps down a quick drink, looking around us. I take my key out, unlock the secondary employee office, and guide him in.

"What's your name, prospect?"

"Uhh. I'd like to go by Fox," he says quietly.

Sitting on the desk facing the two folding chairs, I nod at him to take a seat. "Fox," I drawl out then snort. "We got a bear and a viper, and now we're gonna have a fox. People gonna think we're a bunch of animals."

His lips lift slightly in the corner, as if he's afraid to laugh at my joke, and that makes me chuckle. I shake my head and cross my arms to stare at him.

"Aright, tell me what you got."

Fox clears his throat and pulls out his phone. "He's been splitting us up into groups, and I pulled the location information from my maps. I also cross referenced with other brothers what our assignments were for that day since Dodge and Cowen text different people. Out of six assignments, two of them were redirected elsewhere."

"Where?"

"The bar or the garage."

My jaw tightens. "Elaborate."

"The only pattern I could find is that usually on the days we're supposed to be helping clear the junkyard, he splits a couple of us up to help somewhere else, the bar or the garage."

I stare at the stacks of boxes against the wall, my mind turning over what to do with that information. We've had no discrepancies at the garage, but we've only been checking for money. Pulling out my phone, I send a text to Dodge to double check the inventory of our off-market parts.

"And when you come to the bar, what do you do?" I ask. My hunch tells me something is off with Jack's activities, but I can't place how he's stealing the money if so.

Fox shrugs. "Whatever the floor manager asks me to. It's usually security or stocking."

"Thanks," I get out, rubbing a hand down my face. "Keep me informed."

He nods and looks behind him with a quick glance. "Did you want me to stay here for the day?"

"Yeah. Let me know if Jack reaches out to switch you around, okay?"

Fox agrees and leaves me alone in the quiet office. I slink down into the chair he had occupied and sigh. It hurts to know someone is stealing from us, after everything we've done to build up this town and the families we take care of.

My phone rings and I answer Cowen's call. "What?"

"Where you at? You know Viper's changing your code."

I let out a low laugh. "Yeah, he said he was getting bad vibes. Whatever the fuck that means."

"He's a weirdo, but he's usually not wrong," Cowen says.

Sitting up straight, I lean on my knees. "Hey, can you track someone's movement through their phone?"

"Do we have a tracker on it?" he asks without hesitation.

"Nah, but could you hack into it and get their location if I give you proof of texts and calls."

Cowen is silent for a moment, then sighs. "Not necessarily. It could get me to the closest cell tower it pings off, but that could be a couple mile radius. It just depends."

My shoulders slump. "Alright, not worth the effort then. It was just a thought."

"Got something?" he asks, excited like a puppy hearing his favorite toy.

I blow out a breath that turns into a low chuckle. "Not yet. Following a hunch that may not pan out."

"Let me know if you need anything," Cowen says, hanging up after I thank him. My phone vibrates just as I'm putting it in my pocket and I smirk.

Mikayla

Are you kidding me? You fuck me and gone by morning? You fucking bastard.

...

She's still typing as I text Viper to swipe her phone and laptop as soon as she showers. If she's going to get mouthy, there's gonna be consequences.

Mikayla

It's been a few days since my brother and father fucked me in the clubhouse. I woke up the morning after alone in my bedroom at the family house with care baskets of soaking salts and instructions to take care of myself. Other than that, I haven't seen either of them, and I'm getting more upset with each passing day since they went as far as taking away my cell phone and other devices.

I'm surprised when I'm woken up by the sensation of something hot and wet on my breasts. Blinking, I look down at Gage suckling my nipple on his side with his hand resting on my stomach.

"What are you doing?" I whisper groggily.

His tongue flicks at the taunt bud before he kisses the skin and looks up at me. "Do you think we did it?" he says, his hand flexing.

"What?"

"Knocked you up." His fingers drift and slip between my legs. I'm only wearing an oversized T-shirt. I don't even have underwear on. He seems to have pushed the shirt up to my collarbone, leaving me bare to the room.

"It's too soon to tell."

"I know," he smiles, his eyes glittering with heat. "I guess we'll just have to keep trying."

His finger pushes into me, and my hips arch into his hand. His mouth is back on my nipple, and I cry out when he bites it.

I grab his wrist. "Wait."

He pauses, looking up at me as I scowl and try to push his hand away. "You guys left me for days. You can't just sneak into my room out of nowhere and think I'll open my legs."

His lips pop off my breasts, and he grins, sitting up. His hands grip my thighs, ripping them apart, and he climbs between them. He lets go, resting his palms on either side of my head as he leans over me.

"You wanted to be our whore, did you not?"

I stay silent, and he laughs. He shifts so he's leaning on one arm, undoing his jeans with the other, and pushing them off. He settles between my legs and drops all his weight onto me. I huff out as I lose my breath but wrap my arms around his neck. His hard cock brushes against me, sliding against my shamefully wet folds.

"That means you're ours," he whispers against my skin.

Gage kisses under my jaw, nipping at my chin. His hands slide down my back, cupping my ass and tilting my hips up as he rubs his dick against me. The tip of it bumps into my clit in coordinated strokes.

He lets go momentarily to arrange himself at my entrance before gripping my ass again as he pushes in.

"Ours to *fuck* whenever we want."

I wrap my legs around his hips, my mouth falls open in reaction to the stretch as we stare at each other.

"Ours to *breed*."

He thrusts forward, filling me almost entirely and grinding against my pelvis.

"Ours to *protect*."

His voice turns gravelly, and an unreadable emotion swirls in his eyes. He pumps in and out of me a few times. He pushes as far in as he can, reaching the end of me as he pauses.

"Ours to *love*."

I inhale sharply, and his mouth crashes to mine. It's frantic and passionate. My nails dig into his shoulders as he pounds into me. I cling so hard to him as if I'm trying to crawl into his skin. His breaths are ragged and fan across my neck when he pulls away, grunting with each stroke. His hands squeeze so tightly I know I will be peppered with bruises. But I think he feels the same… like we need more. We need to get so close that there's no beginning or end to the two of us as we fuck.

"Come inside me," I whisper against his lips. Gage groans, picking up his pace.

"Say it again."

"Come inside me." I squeeze down on his cock as my orgasm teeters off the edge. He curses, pumping a few more strokes before hot cum floods me. Our erratic breaths fan across our faces as we stare at each other. His softened gaze makes my chest ache before he rolls off.

I move to my side and place my hand on his chest. "Why'd you guys disappear on me?"

Gage sighs, entangling our fingers together. "We had to figure out what to do."

"With what?"

"You."

I sit up quickly, frowning. "What do you mean with me? I told you I wanted to join the club."

"And I told you it wasn't happening," Gage states, his face impassive.

Scrambling off the bed, I wrap the sheet around me, leaving him naked on the bed. He smirks as he strokes his half mast erection.

"That was the whole point of the other night." I grit out between my clenched teeth.

He shrugs. "We lied."

"You lied?"

Gage pushes off the mattress with a grunt, coming to stand before me as I scowl. "Calm down, Princess."

My mouth drops open as rage starts to boil inside. "Do not fucking tell me to calm—"

"I want to claim you." He smirks, tucking some tangled hair behind my ear.

The fire building inside me disappears, leaving me with warmth around my heart. I breathe out a small gasp. "Claim me?"

Gage nods. "You want to be a part of the club? Then you're mine and *only* mine. You okay with that?"

I nod, unable to say anything and trying hard to contain my smile. My heart is actively trying to escape my chest with how hard it is pounding. I never thought Gage would want me like that.

Gage pulls me into his chest, his hands drifting to squeeze my ass. "You sure? You'll be my old lady. There will never be anyone else for you?"

I rest my head on his shoulder. "Not even Dad?"

Gage goes rigid, his fingers digging into my ass. "Do you want him?"

"I don't know. I've never really thought about him like that. It's only ever been you, but the other night…"

"It was hot," Gage agrees and then lets go, stepping back. He runs a tattooed hand across his jaw. "I would be okay with him, but no one else."

My heart skips a beat. "Gage, I'm not saying—"

"No, I get it. We opened this door, it's not right of me to close it."

Swallowing down the emotion threatening to close my throat, I shake my head and then admit. "I want to be your old lady."

He laughs. "Good because Dad is already telling the council and we need to go in there and put on a show."

"Wait, what?"

"Sorry, Princess. The little private show between the family didn't count," he taunts, his lips curling on one side and a small dimple popping out near his chin. He doesn't seem sorry at all. In fact, his eyes turn heated, and he grabs my shoulders, turning me toward the bathroom.

"Go shower, and then I need to show off my old lady," he says, tapping my ass gently.

I'm tempted to argue with him. Tell him that I don't agree with it, but I would be lying. A hum of excitement runs under my skin at the thought of Gage publicly claiming me like that. So I take a shower, unable to stop smiling.

SHAW

Staring at the men around the table, nerves slide down my spine. It's been a long time since I've felt nervous, but I know what is about to go down is going to have me losing a lot of respect among the men.

I clear my throat and stand. "We've been together a long time now."

The men holler, banging on the table at the nostalgia of the times we've been through. My chest aches, and I run a hand through my beard.

"And I've led this club to a lot of success. I hope you guys take that into consideration with what I'm about to confess."

"What the hell is goin' on, Prez?" Bear grumbles.

"Gage is claiming an old lady today—"

Another round of hollers goes out, and I hold up a hand as I grimace. "He's claiming Mikayla."

Silence falls throughout the room before Scruff smacks a hand on the wooden table. "Mik just barely turned eighteen, she—"

"Nothing happened before she was of age," I confirm.

"So what, your boy just been counting down til midnight if that ain't just as fucked up," Bear sneers.

Anger pulses, and I take a deep breath. "No, it just happened. *Mutually*. They've both expressed this is what they want, and they are consenting adults. He's asking to make her an old fucking lady and that tells you the extent of his feelings."

Bear scoffs again, crossing his huge arms as he stares at me with contempt. I let my own fury show on my face, and I glance at my men.

"That boy has a solid head on his shoulders, and you fucking know that. He's been the driving force behind a lot of what makes this club run, and he doesn't deserve this judgment."

"He's gotta have our votes," Scruff says, a few other men muttering in agreement.

I nod. "Yeah, he does. And what about the time you needed the money to pay off your mother's rent? Who gave it to you so you didn't have to approach the club for a loan?"

Grinning when a few men start to pale at what I'm implying, I turn to Bear. "Or when you needed the cash for your old lady's second rehab attempt."

He shifts in his seat, his face angled down.

"I can go on. I'm sure I can pull an example for each of you fuckers. The point is my family bleeds for this club, and you fucking know this. Whatever makes Gage happy, he fucking deserves it."

I slide into my seat as they're silent, thinking over what I said.

Bear clears his throat. "How's he want to do this? Show or celebration?"

"Show." I smirk, sending Gage a text to bring Mikayla up.

Scruff sits up. "And his second?"

My impish grin deepens. "That's up to Mikayla."

I have no doubt in my mind she'll be choosing me, and they'll just have to accept it. Mostly because it's been years since an old lady has chosen to be fucked into the club while the council watches. Instead, they've chosen a celebration where she flirts with alcohol poisoning.

Gage knocks once before walking in, dragging a smiling Mikayla behind him. He clears his throat, standing at the end of the table.

A small amount of appreciation runs through me at the blank faces the men hold. The previous judgment and apprehension are wiped clean from them.

Gage wraps his arm around Mikayla's waist. "I'm not asking for your permission, she's going to become mine regardless of what you say. But... it would mean a lot to me if you gave us your blessing. I know it might seem a bit odd given the circumstances, but Mikayla has always meant more to me. She never really felt like my sister."

"And you want this fuckwad, Mik?" Bear nods toward Gage.

She smiles, snuggling into his chest. "I do."

Scruff snorts, then smacks his lips. "Alright, get the show on the road."

Gage glares at him and turns Mikayla so her back is facing them. His hand cups her face. "You trust me?"

"Always," she replies instantly.

He pushes her to lie down on the table. Her head rests close to where I'm standing. Gage's hands drift up her dress, resting at her thigh before his gaze locks on Scruff. "Clothes are staying on. She's mine."

Scruff grunts, waving at him to continue and I bite back my smile. It isn't a requirement for Mikayla to be naked, but I'm struggling with them seeing her myself. I'm proud of my son's possessiveness.

Gage looks at me and then slides his hands up Mikayla's dress, pulling her panties down. She fidgets on the table, the nerves obvious as she holds her arms to her chest.

I lean forward. "You okay, Princess?"

She nods, gasping when Gage's hand disappears under her dress again.

His arm pistons between her legs as her eyes roll shut. My cock grows hard at the sound of her wet pussy leaking all over my son's fingers.

He unbuckles his pants, having no shame in pulling out his cock and stroking it.

"You want me to fuck you? Claim you?"

Mikayla looks at him. "Yes."

"Tell him what you want, Princess." I guide her, suppressing my smile at the reference to the night we've already shared.

"I want you to fuck me. Make me yours, Gage."

Gage groans, holding her dress for coverage as he steps forward and slides into her. Mikayla bites down on her lip hard, and I know she's trying to contain any noise.

He starts to pound her hard, unrelenting in his strokes as the slapping of skin and the sloshing of her juices echo in the room. Gage leans forward, one palm on the table next to her, the other collaring her.

"Should I tell the boys how else I'm claiming you?" He kisses her, her legs wrapping around his waist when he thrusts harshly. Her dress starts to slide up, exposing more of her bare legs. A quick glance around shows me that none of the men are even looking there, all eyes on the passionate kiss Gage and Mikayla are sharing.

He pulls back, his fingers dragging down her chest as he stands straighter. Gage's hands grab onto her thighs, pulling her closer to him with a quick tug. "Should I tell them that this is the second load of my cum you're taking today? That your desperate little pussy is just begging to be filled."

Mikayla whimpers. Gage's hand disappears under her dress, and when her body jerks, I can safely assume he's playing with her clit.

"Should I tell them that I've been coming in your fertile cunt, and it's been keeping my seed nice and deep," he whispers, his gaze flicking up to finally acknowledge the room. "Should I tell them that there's no doubt in my mind that come next month, you're gonna be growing my kid in that belly?"

Mikayla nods.

"Good girl. Now choose a second, Princess," he commands.

Her eyes fly open, and she looks immediately at me. "Daddy…"

My chest swells with affection, but I keep my face impassive as the council registers what she says. Bear gives a low chuckle that actually has my shoulders relaxing. It's the type of support I was looking for.

I glance around daring anyone to object as I unbuckle my pants, pulling my hard cock out. "You sure, Mikayla?"

"I'm sure." She nods, reaching out as I step closer to the table. Her hand wraps around my shaft, stroking it as I swipe her dark hair away from her face. Mikayla stretches her neck as her lips wrap around my cock, suckling it gently.

"Jesus," Scruff mutters under his breath. I scowl at him, and he throws his hands up, motioning a zip across his mouth.

Her hand drops as she leans up on her elbow and pulls me further into her mouth as her tongue swirls around me. I stroke the base of my hardened length, wanting desperately to bury myself down her throat. But I can't come in her mouth, the point of this show is only to prove she's comfortable in front of the brothers. Only Gage is allowed to claim her with his cum. Her head bobs as she struggles to stretch her jaw fully around my girth.

"I'm close," Gage warns as if he read where my mind went.

I nod, staring down at Mikayla as I pull out of her small mouth. "Push your tits together, Princess. I'm gonna come on them."

Her fingers pull at the top of the dress, and Gage growls. "Keep them covered."

She cups her breasts, pushing them up as I fuck my fist faster. Leaning forward, I swallow down the groan building in my throat as long white ropes splutter across her tan mounds.

Mikayla gasps as a few more strands land over her chest and neck. Stepping back, I push my half-hard cock back into my jeans as Gage starts to pound into her. A few more strokes, and they moan together as he stills.

I grab a towel, handing it to Gage to clean his woman.

Turning back to the men, I smirk at their appraising glances. "Any objections?"

There's silence for a moment before Gage whispers, "You're all mine, Princess."

GAGE

Grinning, I shake out the leather jacket. I run my fingers over the patch of my name on the back. The thought of her riding bitch with this jacket on her back stating *Property of Gage* makes me hard as fuck. I need to fuck her in this cut as soon as possible. Glancing at the front window, I wonder if she'd allow me to slip it in before her appointment. It's been a few weeks since we fucked her in the office, and she's late. Instead of buying a cheap test from the store, she wants to see her gynecologist and possibly get an ultrasound.

I run up the driveway, closing the front door softly and hanging up the jacket.

"Mik, you ready? Because if you're not, bend over and let me fuck you, Princess," I shout, stomping up the stairs.

She laughs when I enter the bedroom. She's fully dressed and finishing up the last touches of her mascara.

I pout as I take in the white dress flowing around her, glowing against her tan skin. Her dark hair curled down her back. "Dress? We're taking my bike."

She shrugs. "Then don't crash."

"I would prefer you wear jeans."

"They're gonna ask me to take them off. The ultrasound thingy has to be shoved up my vagina since the little bean would be too small to see through my stomach," she explains, sitting on the edge of the bed as she slips on her Doc Martens.

My head snaps back. "What do you mean they're gonna shove something up your pussy?"

"The wand stick that does the ultrasound." Mikayla rolls her eyes. "I don't know. I'm not a doctor. I just googled if I could get one done this early."

I narrow my eyes but let it go for now because I'm excited to show her my gift. Smiling, I step closer and hold out my hand to pull her up from the mattress. She smiles as I cup her face. "I have something for you."

Her crimson-red lips thin out. "I swear if you say your dick..."

I laugh, twisting my fingers into her hair and tilting her head back. "If I say my dick, you'll get on your knees and suck it. Won't you, Princess?"

Her pupils dilate, and her pulse picks up in her neck. "I don't want to be late, Gage."

"Alright. Let's go find out if you're having my baby," I smirk, pulling her out of the room. When we get down the stairs, I step behind her and place my hands over her eyes. I had left the jacket hanging to the left of the front door.

"Gage!" she yelps excitedly, her hands wrapping around my wrists.

I stop us right in front of her gift, and I take a deep breath. She's already said yes, but I'm still nervous to present it to her. This is the start of our forever, a piece she'll always carry with her. I lean into her ear. "I love you, Princess. I think a part of me somehow knew you were always meant to be more."

Mikayla's nails dig into my skin, and her swallow is audible, so I let my hands drop before she can say anything. She inhales sharply, stepping forward and caressing the back of the leather.

"What do you think?" I ask. My stomach churns with nerves. Her putting on that jacket means more than a wedding proposal, it means she accepts me and the club as her forever.

She pulls it down and faces me with tears in her eyes. She holds it out for me to help her put it on, and my heart skips a beat. Grabbing the jacket from her, I shake it and then flip it around so she can slide it on. Mikayla swipes her hair to one side, putting her arms in as I pull it up to rest on her shoulders.

"I love it," she whispers, turning back to me. The emotion reflected on her face has me wanting to tear up myself.

I clear my throat and cup her cheeks. "Even without the claim, you know the club would have taken care of you if anything happened. But this gives me peace from some jackass trying to swoop in and steal you."

She rolls her eyes, smiling. "Don't be stupid, I've only ever seen you."

· ♥ · ♥ · ♥ · ♥ · ♥ ·

She bounces out of the office, waving the tiny ultrasound image in her hand. Her dress swirls around her, and her leather jacket pronouncing her my property stopping right above her ass is making me hard. I bite down on my lip, watching her with a wide smile as I follow behind her. When she reaches my bike, she spins to face me.

"We're having a baby," she says with a grin.

I grab her around her waist, pulling her into my body. "We're having a baby."

"Look at it. It's like a tiny peanut in my belly," Mikayla coos, staring down at the black and white photo.

I take my wallet out and grab the image from her. I fold it and tuck it away before stuffing it back in my pocket. She watches with a pout and I cup her face, kissing her frowning lips once.

"It's for safe keeping," I tell her, slipping my hand down to her ass and squeezing it. "You hungry?"

She kisses me again. "Yeah, I could go for a burger."

Handing over her helmet, I climb on and start the engine as she finishes buckling it in. Mikayla straddles my bike behind me with the expertise one would expect from the president's daughter.

With her chest flush against my back and her legs snug around my hips, she wraps her arms around my waist. I give her clasped fingers a squeeze and then grab the handlebars to walk the bike backwards before shooting out of the parking lot.

Her hold tightens as we drive down the road, and I can feel her cheek pressed against my back. I love riding, but there's something about sharing it with the person you love. When we have a straight shot on the highway, I gun it and her laugh echoes in my ear. I smile, wishing I had more moments of just the two of us like this.

I don't usually love riding with a passenger, but Mikayla is different. She's always been different, even when she was a little girl. The fierce protectiveness I had over her should have frightened me.

As she got older, I became wary of my feelings that grew for her. I threw myself into the club, working to build our future however she stayed in it.

"Gage!" Mikayla shouts, pointing over at a parking lot coming up. I recognize the sign and shake my head, she use to be obsessed with this food. Of course she would be craving it now that she's pregnant with my baby.

As soon as I pull into the lot, she hops off my bike, running up to the food truck and ordering us food. My cock jerks at the claim on her back, and I can't contain the smirk when a guy does a double-take at the jacket. His eyes shift over the parking lot till he finds me and his face pales as he turns back to his food. I chuckle, knowing simple curiosity got the best of him but the power from his fear is addicting.

A few minutes later, Mikayla comes skipping back with a crinkled bag in tow.

"You got it or you want me to hold?" I ask her as she climbs back on.

She scoffs. "I'm good."

With a smile, I drive her to our favorite spot on the cliffs by the beach. The small rest stop is usually used by people traveling with dogs who need to let them out for a quick break while driving down the long pacific coast highway.

Most days it sits empty but the small bench near the railing is always open.

Mikayla jumps off as soon as I park, heading straight to our spot. It's been a couple years since I've taken her here since I made myself scarce when she kissed me on her sixteenth birthday.

She inhales sharply. "God I love the smell of the ocean."

Moving to sit next to her, I grab a burger from the bag and watch the waves wash over the sand. She moves close to me, her thigh brushing against mine.

"You know this is kind of like a date," Mikayla teases.

I look at her with a smirk. "Kind of? Baby, this is about as romantic as I get."

She rolls her eyes. "I guess I'll have to drop hints as per usual."

Shaking my head, I turn back to my food. The peacefulness of nature is not one I get to experience a lot anymore. I stopped camping with Dodge and Jack years ago, instead choosing to stay back and pick up their shifts for the extra cash. It feels nice to slow down and take it in.

"Do you think I'll be a good mom?"

I turn sharply to stare at Mikayla after her abrupt question. Her forlorn look makes my heart ache.

"Of course I do."

Her eyebrows scrunched together. "It's just we don't really have many examples. My mom took off, your mom was never around. Most of the old ladies and their kids kept to themselves."

"The fact that you care about being a good mom already says a lot, Mikayla." I crunch the empty paper from my burger and move close to her. "Shitty parents don't care if they're shitty parents."

"Or they don't know they're shitty parents until one day their kid just stops talking to them," she says with a frown.

I hold out my hand and she grasps it, so I pull her off the bench and into my arms. "Baby, you have so much love to give. I can feel it, you're going to love our child so fiercely."

Mikayla laughs in my chest, tilting her head back to look up at me. "Who knew you have such a sweet side."

I nip at her lips playfully. "And no one ever will, only you."

"Only me," she whispers with a smile. "I like that."

Squeezing her ass, I let go and tangle her fingers with mine. "Let's go home, baby mama," I say as we walk back to my bike.

"So you can love me fiercely in bed?" she teases.

I growl and push her up against my bike as we reach it. I kiss her, pushing everything I feel about her into the kiss. She has to know how much I love her, how much I love our baby. My hands move to her ass, slipping under her dress and grabbing her cheeks.

Kissing down her neck, I lift her onto my bike sideways. She grips onto the seat as I spread her legs and have her feet resting on my shoulders.

"You good?" I ask her as my fingers skim her panties.

She licks her lips. "What are you doing?"

"A date ends with a kiss, does it not? I'm gonna kiss my girl exactly where she's desperate for it." I push her panties to the side and lick up her wet slit. Her juices drench my tongue as I devour her cunt. Mikayla groans, her hold tightening on the seat as her legs shake.

"Gage, *please*," she cries.

I'm not sure what she's begging for but I thumb her clit in gentle circles as I continue to eat her out. It's not long before her trembling stiffens, and she lets out a low moan as her pussy pulses under my tongue. Pulling away, I wipe at my mouth and stand straight to adjust my hard cock.

Just as I'm about to pull it out and plunge inside her, a police cruiser turns into the parking lot. I fix her panties and pull down her dress.

"Come on, Princess. Let's get you home," I say, handing over her helmet and climbing onto the bike before her.

I glance at the police officer as we drive past and only let go of my tension when I notice they don't follow me out. Her arms squeeze me once as we put good distance between us and the beach, and I know it's to say she's with me whatever might have happened.

SHAW

Cowen cracks his neck to the side, sighing before returning to his laptop. I rub my eyes, tired of staring at the constant numbers and lines. Shoving the papers away from me with a groan, I lean back into my chair.

"I'm gonna murder the fucker who is wasting my time like this," I seethe through clenched teeth.

A hollow laugh barks out of Cowen's throat. "It's kind of fun, like a predator hunting its prey. I have to try multiple tactics to hopefully catch a pattern."

"We've been over these reports so many times, I'm beginning to think I can recite them from memory."

Cowen smirks and then his jaw tightens. "We'll find the bastard."

The door of my office swings up, Mikayla plowing through with a giant grin. Her gaze flickers to Cowen before returning to me as she skips to my desk.

"Hi *Daddy*," she says with a slight whine. My cock perks up instantly.

Cowen slams his laptop closed. "Okay, that's my cue to leave."

"Aww. Don't let me kick you out. Be wherever you need to be, it's not like it would be the first time you've caught us," Mikayla says with a saucy wink.

His mouth parts and he blinks at her, his face blank as if lost in thought. My eyebrows pinch together. It's like she short-circuited his brain.

"Cowen?" I prompt.

Shaking his head, he looks over at me. "We've been looking at everything with the assumption everyone is where they're supposed to be. I have an idea." He stands, giving Mikayla a nod and leaves the room while closing the door behind him.

She watches him leave with a frown before glancing back at me.

"What you doing here, Princess?" I grin as she walks closer and sits on the edge of my desk. I wheel my chair a few inches forward, resting my hand on her thigh and playing with the bottom of her dress. "Where's Gage?"

"He dropped me off. Said he needed Viper and Dodge for something and he'll come get me in a few hours," she says, biting down on her lip. She looks down at her curled fist, a paper wrinkling inside. "And I wanted to show you something."

I swallow, my heart beating faster as she unfolds the ultrasound and holds it out for me. I take it from her, my eyes misty at the image.

"Our baby," Mikayla whispers. A sharp pang jabs me in the heart, but I nod.

Smiling, I place it on my desk. It hurts to look at, but also fills me with overwhelming joy. "I didn't think it would happen so fast."

She laughs, and rolls her eyes. "Gage keeps making comments about super sperm."

"Yeah, that sounds like him." I chuckle.

Mikayla bites down on her lip. "Are you happy?"

My head jerks back and I stare at her. "Yeah, Princess. I am. Why you ask?"

She shrugs, looking away. "You just don't come around as much as Gage."

"I'm a busy man. I usually don't have time till way past your bedtime," I tell her, my fingers tracing up her thighs.

Her hand catches mine and pulls it closer to the apex between her legs. "I wouldn't mind you still coming in the middle of the night."

"Yeah?" I breathe out, my cock growing harder at her implication.

I slide her more towards the center of my desk, pulling her ass near the edge. Spreading her legs, I push her dress up till it pools in her lap. My fingers glide up her inner thighs and towards her pussy.

"I can smell how wet you are," I say with a sharp inhale.

Mikayla lets out a slight gasp as I swipe across her soaked slit. "Gage, he—before... Oh god."

Pushing two fingers into her, I glance up at her face. "He what?"

"H-he ate my pussy at the park," she gets out in a single breath before moaning as I start working my fingers inside her.

"Yeah? He got this pussy all nice and wet for me? Your little pussy is all sensitive because it's already come?"

Mikayla leans back, her fingers gripping the edge of the desk as her breasts jut out from the arch of her chest. "Yes, Daddy. *Please.*"

I unbuckle my belt, unzip my jeans, and pull out my hard cock. Stroking it up, I see the pre-cum leaking and add another finger into her tight pussy. I don't think she'll ever adjust to taking my size in one go.

"Hop on my cock, Princess," I say, dropping my hand and pulling her off the desk as her arms wrap around my neck for balance. I notch myself at her entrance, and we both let out a small hiss when my head pops into her snug hole and she starts to sink down on my dick.

My hands cup her ass, and I spread my legs wider so she can adjust her position.

"Pull your dress down. Let me see your tits."

She does what I demand and I suck the hard nipple of one her perky breasts into my mouth. Her pussy clenches around me and she slides down a few more inches.

"Oh god. You're so big," she groans.

I growl, biting down on her tit. I grip her hips and thrust up. "Take it, baby. It's all for you."

She cries out as my entire cock is shoved into her tight cunt. Her gushing pussy drips down onto my balls, and I take comfort in knowing that she's wet enough that she's not in pain.

My gaze roams over her flushed face and I throb inside her. She's so goddamn beautiful it physically pains me.

I wrap my hand around her long hair, pulling her head back further.

Thrusting harder, I growl into her neck. "You like sitting on Daddy's cock?"

She rocks her hips with my pumps, trying to keep up. "*Yes, yes, yes.*"

"Beg for Daddy's cum, Princess." The slick wet warmth of her tight hole is gripping my cock so hard, I'm not sure she'll ever let go of it. Her nails dig into my shoulders so hard that I barely feel pinches of pain as she punctures my skin.

She's trembling as her release builds. "Please," Mikayla begs, her whiny voice turning me on. "*Please* come inside me, Daddy."

"Fuck," I curse as I empty my entire load inside her tight pussy. She jerks with the first spray of my cum and then she pulses around me as she follows me into ecstasy. My head drops into the valley of her breasts as we pant, coming down from our high.

I knead the flesh of her hips as her breathing calms and then look up at her. My cock softens in her pussy, causing our mess to drip down, but I don't give a fuck.

Her eyes are hooded as she stares down with a soft smile. I desperately want to kiss her, but my phone goes off, interrupting the moment. I groan as she climbs off my lap and I want to kill whoever is calling. She chuckles as she grabs the paper towels from the desk, wiping herself clean as I scowl.

"Don't go far. I don't like you getting rid of my cum," I say.

She bites down on her lip, flashing me a heated look as she nods and drops to the couch.

"What the fuck you want," I say, answering the damned device.

Mikayla

Twisting my body in the mirror, I rub my hand over the small bump protruding just above my underwear. A strange giddiness runs through me at the sight of it. Even after the ultrasound photos they handed us weeks ago, it didn't feel as real as it does now. I'm growing a baby. I'm growing *their* baby. My cheeks are warm, and my smile is bright with happiness.

"Jesus," Gage breathes out behind me, and I look at him through the mirror, but his eyes are on my belly. "It just popped out overnight."

I roll my eyes and turn to him. "Don't say that stuff to a pregnant woman."

He smirks, walking to me and cradling my face in his hands. "You're my sexy little mama."

He kneels before me, kissing down the bump and rubbing his hands across it. His fingers hook into my panties, pulling them down my legs. I hold onto his shoulders as I step out of them. His hands glide up my thighs, squeezing my ass as he looks up at me before standing.

"Get on your hands and knees," he commands, nodding at the bed. I skip to the mattress, already wet. I'm insatiable for him.

I climb on, presenting my pussy as he steps up behind me. His jeans are rough against my skin as he rocks me against his erection. "You have any idea how much I fucking *live* for you?"

My breath catches and warmth spreads in my chest. He unzips in his pants, and I feel the familiar stretch of his tip breaching my entrance as he slides into me.

"That kiss when you were sixteen. You took my soul with it," he continues as he slowly thrusts. His hands drift from my hips to my belly. His fingers gently caress the taunt skin, and my throat burns with emotion.

"And to know you're having my baby. Seeing your belly swollen with my child… leaves me breathless." He pushes into me harder, picking up his pace as he rubs my stomach.

"God, it turns me on. Just the thought that I filled you with my cum and you're pregnant makes me so fucking hard I can barely walk."

"Gage," I moan, my fists clenching at the sheets as I rock back into him. "Please."

He fucks me relentlessly; the sound of our skin slapping echoes in the room. "Touch yourself," he demands. "Come on my cock, Princess."

I press my face into the mattress, leaning on my shoulder to reach back. A thrill runs through me at the thought that he doesn't want to let go of my belly as he pummels me with his dick. The fact that he is so turned on by my pregnant body brings me closer to my impending orgasm. I barely have to rub a few circles before I clench down on him, screaming as my legs tremble from the force of it.

Gage moves faster, chasing his own release through mine. "Fuck, fuck. You feel so good. *Every. Damn. Time.*" The last few words are each emphasized with deep thrusts till I feel the heat of his cum flooding into me.

My pussy clenches, the greedy hussy dragging his seed deeper inside me. Even after getting knocked up immediately, Gage coming inside makes me throb. The way he fucks me is raw and animalistic as if he can't control himself.

He collapses on top of me, shifting to the side and pulling me into his chest. "I don't think I'll ever have enough of you."

"I hope not," I tease and tap his hand to let go of me. I climb over him and head to the bathroom. "Wanna shower with me?"

"Nah, I'll grab one later."

Rolling my eyes, I shower quickly, not wanting him to be alone for long. A bored Gage is a dangerous Gage; he'll find something to occupy his time, and I need to get out of this house.

He's resting on the bed, watching me with a smile as I slip on the tight dress. It's light blue with small yellow daisies and shows off my small bump.

"You have me all day, Princess. What do you want?"

I blush, knowing he's hinting at another round, but my hand rubs at my belly. "I want to get some things for the little peanut."

His eyebrows raise. "You don't want to wait until we know what we're having."

"Nope, I'll just get some neutral colors till then," I smile.

He groans. "Are you talking about clothes shopping?"

I laugh, moving to put on my boots. "Yes, and I want to look around at some other stuff. Babies require a lot. I need to get an idea of what we need."

"I think Dad said something about shit in storage," Gage offers, and I try to withhold my grimace. I wasn't against hand-me-downs, but it's been over two decades since Gage was a baby. Who knows what that stuff looks like?

He must catch my look, and he leans over, grabbing my chin and kissing my lips. "I think Dodge wanted to grab something out of there. Maybe some stuff can go missing." He winks and stands, grabbing both our jackets and helping me into mine.

"Let's go shopping, Princess."

· ♥ · ♥ · ♥ · ♥ · ♥ ·

I feel uncontained joy stepping into the baby boutique. I've seen it downtown multiple times, but never had the need to go into it. The associates greet us with large smiles when we walk through the door, which is another welcoming sight. Most would take in our leather and turn up their noses.

"Hello! Are you guys looking for anything in particular or just browsing?" a tiny blonde asks, walking up to us with a clipboard.

Gage drops his arm over my shoulder. "Yeah. Do you have a tiny motorcycle for kids? I gotta teach 'em young."

I smack his stomach and shake my head at the associate. "He's joking. We just wanted to browse the clothes. It's never too early to start the stockpile."

She giggles, sneaking peeks at Gage but trying to keep her attention on me. I can respect her attempt at being respectful to me and not ogling my baby daddy, even though he's ridiculously hot.

"Oh! Do you guys have books about pregnancy for a clueless daddy?" I ask sweetly.

Gage groans, his fingers squeezing at my arm. "I hate reading."

"That's too bad." I look at him, fluttering my eyelashes. "Don't you care about everything I'm going through?"

He narrows his eyes. "Don't make that face."

The associate giggles again. "The books are on the far right wall, and most of the newborn clothes are going to be on the racks over there."

I tell her thanks and pull Gage toward the clothes. His hand pinches my ass as he follows, and I throw him a scolding look over my shoulder.

"Behave yourself."

He smirks and says, "Around you? Never."

Gage actually isn't a bad partner to shop with. It's like the minute his eyes latch onto the first onesie, a switch flips, and suddenly he's in extreme daddy mode. While I only planned to get an outfit for the baby to wear home from the hospital, Gage's arms are now full.

Even the associate's eyes widen when she sees the multiple blankets, burp rags and clothes ranging up to 9 months laid out on the counter.

"I think you enjoyed shopping more than I did," I tease him.

Gage smiles, and rubs my little bump. "Gotta take care of my girls."

The associate makes a cooing noise as she rings us up and I roll my eyes. "You don't even know if it's a girl."

"Wishful thinking?" He chuckles, not even glancing at the final total as he swipes his card.

"Thank you! Make sure to come again before the baby is born." Her cheeks turn red as soon as the words leave her mouth.

Gage snickers, and I smack his arm. Smiling, I thank her and hand the bags over to him.

"Don't even make a comment," I hiss at him as I move quickly away from the register.

Gage laughs loudly as he wraps his arm around me, and we walk out the door, one hand flexing on my bump and his other arm full of bags.

"Mikayla?"

I tense, looking at my old best friend. "Talia?"

Her eyes drift to where Gage is holding me, and her face twists into a judgmental scowl. I tilt my chin up, knowing whatever is about to come out of her mouth will be nasty.

"That certainly was quick, wasn't it?"

Gage lets go, coming to stand next to me. "What the fuck did you just say?"

Talia scoffs. "Come on, Gage. You can't supposedly be happy that your club knocked up your sister."

"Shut up, Talia. You're jealous that none of the guys want you. You were always the first to talk about how hot they are." My fists clench.

"And for the record, I am happy. I love Mikayla, and I'll love our child," Gage says, his tone leaving no argument.

"Isn't he your brother?" another voice exclaims, and I only just notice the man standing next to Talia, their hands clasped together. I glance at that and then at Sean's face. The skin on his neck turns red, and he lets go of her. Talia scowls at him before turning back to us.

"Gage, really?"

I smirk, moving to grab onto Gage's arm. "He even made me his old lady."

Talia flinches. We both know how many times she gushed about being Gage's old lady. Though she was my best friend at the time, I never did like that she had set her eyes on Gage. It was one of the reasons I stupidly tried to kiss him when I was sixteen, needing to stake a forbidden claim before Talia tried.

"Wait, you got knocked up by your brother?" Sean exclaims.

Gage goes rigid, and I'm tempted to let him kick the judgmental prick's ass.

"He's not my real brother, dumbass."

Talia laughs. "Might as well have been. I mean, he took you to school more times than Shaw ever did."

Gage pushes me behind him and steps closer to the two people I once considered friends. "You got something to say, you say it to me. Got it? You keep your goddamn mouths shut to Mikayla because I swear to god, if I find out you guys upset her, I'll fucking kill you."

My eyes widen. I grab his hand. "He's joking."

Sean pales, pulling Talia away from us. "We won't say anything to Mikayla. Don't come near us, or I'll call the police." He pulls on Talia harder when she goes to speak, jerking her across the street.

"You can't just threaten people," I hiss.

Gage faces me, his eyes still hard with anger. "I didn't like what they were saying, especially to you."

I smile, stepping into his chest, and his arms wrap around me. "It doesn't matter what people say, okay? It doesn't bother me. At the end of the day, it's just me, you, and the baby."

He sighs. "You still want to get more shopping done, or you want to go home?"

"Home. I think that's enough peopling today."

SHAW

My jaw aches from how hard I'm clenching it. I shuffle through the papers again and lift my eyes to meet Cowen's. "Video?"

"Every single time," he says with a nod, then rubs at his jaw. His gaze darkens. "I got a hold of his laptop last night."

I lean back into my chair with crossed arms. "And you found the money?"

"No, I found what he's spending his money on. Shaw—" Cowen swallows, his stare dropping to the table. "It's bad."

My stomach turns. "In what way?"

Cowen shakes his head. "Like he shouldn't be around any schools or playgrounds."

I suck in a sharp breath through my teeth. "He's a fucking dead man."

"You should talk to Gage first. There's—" His mouth slams shut. "Just trust that Gage would want a pound of his flesh."

A sick feeling swirls in my chest, aware of what Cowen is saying without speaking it aloud. I want him to confirm, but close my eyes to calm down. If there's anything from when Mikayla was younger, I won't be able to control myself from walking downstairs and putting a bullet between his eyes.

"Alright. Thanks for everything you do, Cowen," I say, standing and clapping him on his shoulder.

He nods and grips my arm. "Tell Gage that I want to come with."

I grimace. "You sure? You usually don't want to get your hands dirty."

"I hate that I've gotten so content that I let this slip by."

Pulling Cowen under my arm, I hug him to my side. "It's not your responsibility but I'm glad to have you along for the ride."

He chuckles, pushing me off him. "Whatever, Old Man. All I'm saying is this is a family and we should all be looking out for each other. We've relied too much on you and Gage and maybe it's time for that to change."

I understand what he's saying, but it's hard to let go of something you built from the ground up. It's hard enough to hand it over to my own son and I trust him more than I trust myself.

"I'll let Gage know tonight. Expect a call from him," I say and grab the paperwork off the desk to take home.

Cowen smirks. "See ya later, Prez."

Gage looks up from the couch where he's lounging with a book as I walk in the back door. I nod toward the stairs. "She asleep?"

"Yeah, she was having trouble, so she took some medication."

I pause. "Like medication to stay asleep?" My cock hardens at the idea lingering in my mind.

Gage raises an eyebrow. "Yes?"

Grinning, I head up the steps to their room, and I hear Gage quietly following behind me. When I open the door to the room, the moonlight drifting from the window gives Mikayla a luminous look over her bare skin. The white panties glow, and the tight tank top leaves nothing to the imagination.

I tilt my head as I step closer to the bed, thankful she has opted to sleep over the covers. Climbing into the bed, I push her legs apart and turn her more onto her back. She sighs, moving easily. Gage comes to stand near the pillows, watching her with the same admiration as me.

"Our whore whenever we want, right?"

He grins, his heated gaze sliding down her body more provocatively. "She's probably all wound up too. She wanted to get off before bed, but I told her no."

Raising an eyebrow, I take my shirt and jeans off, leaving me in my tight briefs. "You told her no?"

"She was being a brat. I get pregnancy hormones, but she doesn't need to scream at me because I chose the wrong cheese for her salad."

I suck my lips in, trying not to laugh. "We have a long way to go, son. I don't think withholding sex is the answer."

Gage shrugs. "Believe me, it hurts me more than her."

"I was just going to look at her while I got off, but I can't have my Princess ending the day unsatisfied."

Leaning over, I brush my fingers down her thighs, tracing up to her covered pussy. "You got your knife on you?"

Gage reaches into his back pocket and hands me the blade. I click it open and slide my fingers under each side of her panties, lifting them off her body and cutting through the material.

"She'll be mad you ruined her clothes," Gage says, shrugging off his own shirt and jeans.

I shrug. "Then buy twice as much to replace them. Here, free those perky tits." I return his knife and focus back on the glistening folds before me.

Running my finger through them, I gather up her wetness before pushing two fingers into her pussy. Mikayla's eyelids flutter a bit, but otherwise, no response.

"How far are you taking this?" Gage asks, licking his lips.

I pump slowly, scissoring my digits open to stretch. "The only place I'm coming is right here."

He nods, stroking his hard cock before moving to squeeze her breasts. "She'd probably be pissed if she woke up covered in cum."

"Look how swollen her clit is. Think we can get her off?" I smirk.

I lean forward, sucking it into my mouth. Mikayla's chest rises and falls faster as I continue to play with her pussy. Gage alternates between pinching and twisting at her hard nipples as she starts to tighten around my fingers. I pick up my pace, flicking at her swollen bud.

Her legs tremble as her pussy flutters around my fingers, a soft whimper exhales from her lips.

"Who knew she could be so quiet?" Gage teases.

Grabbing her thighs, I pry her legs open further and stroke my cock. It hardens as I rub my leaking head across her sopping wet folds. Lining up to her hole, I push in slowly. Even with her relaxed state, I know I'll be stretching her tight pussy.

"Fuck," I whisper, staring down at where I'm disappearing into.

Gage grunts, his hand moving faster as he watches me. "You should have seen her today. Her stomach had the perfect little bump."

My cock throbs, thrusting further. Her warmth pulls me in as I try to imagine what he's saying.

"Yeah?"

He nods. "All swollen with my baby."

"Or mine," I taunt, holding her knees up as I start to pump in and out of her without disrupting her slumbering body. Mikayla staying asleep as I fuck her has my cock swelling, bringing me to the cusp of my release. I'm not sure if it's the thought of her leaking my cum all night or her belly growing round that has me coming. I groan, my head tilting back as I splurt her insides with my seed. A small part of me wishes I could get her pregnant too.

Catching my breath, I pull out after the last pulse and roll to the side. Gage settles between her legs, pushing into her with a quick thrust.

I climb off the bed, grab a towel from the bathroom, and clean myself. Grimacing at the sight of my son squeezing his ass cheeks as he fucks Mikayla, I turn away. I grab my clothes as Gage picks up his pace, uncaring as her breasts bounce with each pump. His deep moan comes with a few more pumps, and his palms slam on either side of her head as he rocks his hips into her.

"The whole point is to keep her asleep, dumbass." His head snaps up to me, and he flips me off as he pulls out of her.

Handing him the towel as he moves off the bed, he cleans himself and pulls on his clothes. I clean the excess cum leaking from her puffy red pussy and tuck the sheet over her bare sleeping body.

I kiss her temple and nod toward the door. "Let's go back downstairs. I need to tell you about what we found."

He follows me to the kitchen and I grab a beer for us.

Swallowing some of it down, I clench my jaw. "Cowen found him."

Gage tenses, setting the bottle down. "Who? How?"

"He was able to trace the money to two separate accounts... in Jack's name."

He closes his eyes, his fist clenching, and takes a deep breath. "We're sure it's Jack?"

I nod, finishing my beer, and then holding out my phone for Gage to take. "Here. Cowen is printing out copies, but I needed to show you tonight. I think he and Dodge are about to leave for their annual trip soon."

Gage mutters they are as he grabs the phone. We stand in silence as he looks through all the evidence of Jack's betrayal. Years of fraudulent charges to accounts and him keeping the money. When Gage's face pales, I know he's gotten to the worst of it. He slams the phone on the counter, breathing heavily.

"I'll take care of it," he growls out.

Frowning, I try to pat his shoulder, but he pulls away from me. "Son, let's take a day and think this through. He doesn't know that we know."

Gage shakes his head. "No, he's a part of *my* crew. I'll fucking handle it."

"Son—"

He turns to me, his eyes wild. "This isn't a fucking discussion anymore. He was my responsibility; this is on me. I have to make my amends with the club."

I bristle at his tone. "Watch who you're fucking talking to, boy."

Gage's throat bobs. "I need to do this."

"Alright. You'll let me know if you need help?" I ask, my body aching from the stress of the entire situation.

He nods and grabs his cut hanging off the chair before pausing. "Will you stay here with her? I need to know she's safe and I'm taking Viper."

"Of course."

Gage sighs before smirking. "There are some pregnancy books on the coffee table. In case you need a refresher, old man."

GAGE

"Fuck," Dodge whispers, glancing at the paperwork. His eyes water before he hands it back. "I don't understand why he didn't just ask for the money. I would have loaned it to him."

My jaw clenches and my stomach drops as I push one more piece of paper to him. Dodge reads it over before crumpling it and punching the wall. He punches it again and then rests his forehead against it. His shoulders shake, and I wait for him to get it all out. Jack has been stealing money because he doesn't want to admit to the photos and videos he's been purchasing on the dark web.

"I'm sorry, brother," I whisper, patting Dodge on the back. He and Jack have been best friends since they were in diapers.

Dodge clears his throat, turning to face me with his head low. "You look through the files?"

"Cowen did."

"Was... was my baby girl in there?" His voice breaks, and my throat aches with my own emotions.

"Not in any that Cowen found."

Dodge releases a long breath and blinks up at me, his red-lined eyes burning with anger and disgust. "What's the plan?"

"Bury the motherfucker."

He nods, pulling out his phone. "Let me call him."

I grab his hand. "Nah, no traces. When's the last time you spoke or texted him?"

Dodge frowns. "I think like two days ago. You know how I am on long work days."

"Good," I nod, texting a few more of our crew. "That's good. He's already distanced himself from most of the club. It was just you, and I'm not putting you at any risk."

His jaw tics. "Don't sideline me. I need to be a part of it."

"Do you? You have the most to lose if we get caught."

Dodge growls. "So do you. You got a goddamn baby on the way, don't ya? So we don't get caught."

Our gazes don't stray from each other, and both our eyes water.

"Forever, brother," I say, holding out my hand. Dodge grabs it and pulls me into his chest, his hand clapping me on the back.

"Forever."

We let go and step back. I nod at the door, hearing the rumbling of bikes as the rest of the crew nears Dodge's house. I had sent Viper to round them up without a call as I grabbed the papers from Cowen's. "Let's go. We got a long night ahead of us."

We find Jack in the back of the clubhouse. I kick the door, causing it to swing open and slam into the wall. He and one of the clubwhores break apart.

"Get lost, Daisy." I catch her arm when she starts to scurry past. "You don't remember anything. You were with me the whole night if anyone ever asks."

Her throat bobs as she swallows, and she nods. One of the men hands her a shirt as she makes her way down the hallway.

Jack scrambles off the bed with a glare. "What the fuck? You could have—"

I squeeze his neck as I slam him into the wall. "You thought we wouldn't figure it out."

He tries to gurgle out a reply, so I tighten my grip. His face is starting to turn red and he tries to push me away. Dodge steps up behind me, and Jack's pleading gaze falls to him.

"Why?" is all Dodge asks. I let go of Jack.

He sputters and coughs as he slides to the ground. "W-what are you talking about?"

My boot connects to his face with a sickening crack. Jack's head flies back, blood spraying as he falls onto his back.

"Try again, stupid fuck. We know everything. Every lie that falls from your mouth only prolongs your death."

He turns, panting as he comes up to his hands and knees. Blood drips onto the floor as his head hangs. My lips turn in disgust at the sight of his limp dick swinging. I grab the sheet from the messy bed and throw it at him.

"Cover yourself. I don't want to stare at that disgusting shit."

Dodge kneels down next to Jack. "Why?"

Jack turns to him, the skin under his eyes already darkening. "I had to."

"Because you were forced or because you couldn't afford to pay the prices you needed for your vice?"

He pales, shaking his head, and a hiccuped sob falls from his swelling lips. "I can't help it. There's something wrong with me."

I look behind me to Cowen, who is watching over it all with a grave expression. His gaze locks with mine and he shakes his head. That's all I need to know that Jack has been buying the worst of it and will probably offend soon.

"Yeah... I'm sure you tried really hard not to look," I say.

Dodge stands, rolling his shoulder forward. "He hasn't even bothered trying to apologize, tells me all I need to know."

"No! No, wait. I'm sorry. Please, Dodge. Don't let them do this. You're my cousin, we're family." he pleads.

Dodge spits at him. "The fact we share blood sickens me."

"Is that how you really want to go out? Begging on the ground like the pathetic piece of shit you are?" I taunt as one of the men behind me hands me a knife.

I nod to Dodge and Cowen. "Hold him down. He doesn't deserve to wear our patch into the afterlife."

Jack tries to stand, but Dodge and Cowen pounce on him, pushing him on his stomach. He squirms, trying to buck them off. I haunch down, tracing our club's logo on his right shoulder with the tip of the knife. Jack flinches at the cold of the metal, an incoherent blubbering mess before Cowen pushes his face into the carpet to silence him.

"If you think this will hurt, imagine what it will feel like when we cut off your dick," I whisper down to Jack. I pinch right above the tattoo, pull on it, and bring the knife down, starting to skin our brand from him. He lets out an ear-piercing wail as Dodge and Cowen tighten their holds. Blood pools down my hands and his back as I pull the flap of skin away, holding it up for the men to see. I stand, and one of the crew holds out a bag for me to throw it in.

"You all know why he's been stripped. Dodge gets the final blow, but you're all welcome to a piece." My gaze lingers on the gathered men inside the room, and I know a few more linger in the hallway.

I walk into the attached bathroom to wash my hands, and I take a deep breath as Jack's screams start up again. Watching the blood swirl in the white porcelain bowl under the water, I allow myself one moment of grief for the man I thought was a brother. Then I push him out of my mind and exhale in relief, knowing the long nights of research and waiting are over. I can focus entirely on Mikayla and our baby.

Mikayla

Gage and Shaw basically disappeared overnight. I haven't seen them in days, and I'm starting to get worried. When I wake up for the fifth morning in a row without my pussy aching from being used overnight or a heavy tattooed arm over my waist, I form a plan.

I change into jeans, a tight t-shirt that gets caught on my belly, and my boots before heading downstairs. Viper looks up from where he's watching TV on the couch as I head to the kitchen.

Pulling out a bowl, I grab the ingredients to make cinnamon rolls and ignore the rustle of footsteps and the scrape of a stool by the counter. After a few minutes, Viper clears his throat.

So let the games begin. I push out my bottom lip, set the bowl down and look up at him with watery eyes. "I was going to try to bake something, b-but…"

"But what?" he asks, looking over the ingredients. I know he knows what they could potentially make.

"But there's never anyone else to enjoy them. Shaw and Gage are always gone." My lip quivers and I wipe away a fake tear.

"What are you going to make?"

A smile threatens to take over, but I battle it down. "Cinnamon rolls."

He licks his lips. "With the nutella?"

I nod slowly and then sigh. "With the nutella. It's just a lot of work to not be appreciated."

Viper hits his chest with his fist. "Mik, I'd appreciate the fuck out of it."

Smiling, I lean over the counter. "Really?"

He nods quickly.

I cock my head to the side as my grin falls off. "They leave you here an awful lot, don't they?"

Viper stills, his eyes narrowing as he takes in the change of my expression. "They trust me."

"But like there's no cameras to prove if I were to claim you touched me?"

His jaw tics and he shakes his head. "Gage knows I would never."

"But the doubt would be there." He stares at me, disappointment bleeding into his eyes and I lean back.

"What do you want, Mikayla?" he asks, disdain evident in his tone.

I purse my lips. "I want to go to the clubhouse."

"Alright." He moves to slide off the stool and I wave for him to stay.

"I'm making your cinnamon rolls first, duh."

Viper rolls his eyes, a small smile lifting at the corner of his mouth and sits back down.

· ♥ · ♥ · ♥ · ♥ · ♥ ·

I feel sick as Viper pulls into the clubhouse parking lot, turning the truck off and glancing at me warily. "You should let me call them again."

Shaking my head, I grab the handle. "No. If they cared, they would answer on the first ring."

He sighs, climbing out of the truck with me. "Just make sure to tell Gage this was your idea when he tries to kick my ass."

My lips curl into a faint smile. "I'll tell him I blackmailed you, you had no choice."

It's not overly busy this time of day, in comparison to the gatherings in the evenings. But there's still stragglers just off the night shift coming in or the early risers getting ready for the day. Conversation falls silent when I step in the door and they all look over at me.

The previous nausea returns to my stomach and I swallow down the bile threatening to rise. "I'm looking for Gage. Anyone seen him?"

A few of the men shake their heads, exchanging glances that have me suspecting they're lying.

I straighten my shoulders and narrow my eyes at them. "If someone doesn't tell me where my goddamn baby daddy is at, you'll fucking regret it."

One of the clubwhores scrambles forward, her face pale. I can't remember her name to save my life, but she could be new for all I know. I've been barred from coming here much the past couple of years. "He's been out all day, Mik. But he's been here the past couple nights," she says, holding up her hands as if to calm me.

Nausea claws at my throat, threatening to spew my feelings. I take in her tight tank top and short jean skirt. It's not anything out of the ordinary for the women of the clubhouse, but jealousy burns in my chest at how tiny she looks.

"With you? He was with you?" I ask with a shaky breath.

Her eyes widen and her mouth slacks. "Uh—uhm. He's been—"

She doesn't answer as her stuttering stalls out and she looks back at the group standing silent behind her.

I grab the empty beer bottle on the table next to me and throw it. It's way off base and one of the men step aside as it shatters against a stool. Tears streak down my cheeks as my body shakes in fury, and I reach to grab something else to throw..

"It's a fucking yes or no question. Is Gage sleeping with you?!" I scream.

GAGE

"And the farm?" Shaw asks.

Bear nods. "Confirmed the pigs have been fed."

I exhale out a breath, glad for it to be over. Dodge is staring at a blank spot in the wall with a desolate expression. They grew up together and I knew this would hit him the hardest.

"You okay?"

Dodge nods, swallowing and looking up at his dad. "Yeah, the world is better off."

"Still your family. I know it hurts," Shaw says, tugging at his beard as he leans back in his chair.

Cowen clears his throat. "I've been looking into some systems to implement in all the businesses. To make bookkeeping easier and catch things faster."

"If it's all one system, wouldn't that be easier for someone to hack," I say with a frown.

He sends me an incredulous look, as if daring someone to try to hack him. "Potentially, but—"

Glass shattering has us all dropping our boots onto the floor and then the following screeching has me out the door. Running from the council room, I jog down the stairs and lock eyes with a volatile Mikayla. Her swollen face and red eyes break my heart as her mouth quivers.

"Baby? What's wrong?"

She points a finger at a frightened Daisy. "Are you sleeping with her?"

My head jerks back before I scowl and storm over to her. She tries to move back, but I catch her jaw. "What did you just say?"

Mikayla glares at me. "I said are you fucking that club-whore while leaving your pregnant old lady at home."

"That's it," I growl. I bend and pick her up. Her legs immediately wrap around my waist and her nails dig into my neck.

"Put me down!" she yells.

I'm tempted to bite down on the small curve where her neck meets her shoulder, but I know I'm too angry not to break the skin. She squirms as I carry her up the stairs and to Shaw's large suite. Slamming the door open with my booted foot, I barely refrain from tossing her onto the bed and instead set her down carefully since she's carrying precious cargo.

Shaw follows in behind us, shutting the door as I step back from the mattress. Mikayla looks between us with watery eyes. Crossing my arms, I glare down at her.

"Explain what that was," I say through gritted teeth.

Tears pour down her face and she breaks out into a sob. Her shoulders shake. Shaw moves to step around me but I slam my hand into his chest.

"No, don't comfort her," I say. His eyes narrow, and his jaw tics like he's about to protest, but her little voice speaks up.

"I'm s-sorry. It's t-the hormones," she cries.

I sigh and kneel before her, my hands barely touching her knees. "Baby. You know the clubwhores don't touch the claimed men. Why would you accuse Daisy of that?"

Her chin trembles and her eyes lift to mine. "I don't know."

"You think I would cheat on you?"

Mikayla shakes her head, wiping at her tears and using the sleeve of her shirt to wipe her nose. "No. She said she was with you at night and I just lost my mind."

Shaw sits onto the bed next to her. "She said she was with Gage?"

Her eyebrows scrunch together. "I think so?"

I exchange a glance with him. We'll have to check with her to make sure what exactly she said to Mikayla. When we told her to claim she was with me the night we took care of Jack, I didn't mean to the woman carrying my child. But at the same time, Mikayla knows how we operate. The club women are here to be shared with the single men in exchange for all their expenses paid. They don't fuck with taken men, we don't do that drama shit.

"You're gonna go back down there and apologize, ya hear me?"

She nods and tries to get up, but I push her back onto the mattress and I stand. Unbuckling my pants, I smirk. "After you apologize to us."

Mikayla's head jerks back, her mouth parting. "A-apologize for what?"

"For disrespecting him in front of the men. For accusing him of cheating when he's very publicly claimed you," Shaw says.

Pulling out my cock, I stroke myself once and dip my chin. "Suck my cock between your lips."

She leans forward, licking at my tip and I groan. I'll never get used to the feeling of her mouth on me. Shaw moves behind her, pulling at her jacket. She shrugs it off and his hands immediately knead her breasts through her shirt. I pull back, smearing her saliva down my shaft.

"Strip."

Shaw helps her up and unbuttons her pants as she drags her t-shirt over her head. Her baby bump is becoming more pronounced with each passing week and I'm obsessed with seeing it. As she unclips her bra, Shaw slides off her panties.

"Hands and knees, Princess," I tell her, directing her towards the bed as I remove the rest of my clothes.

Mikayla crawls on the mattress, looking like the absolute goddess she is. Her long dark hair hangs in front of her face and her plump ass is begging to be smacked as she moves. She positions herself till she faces me on her palms and knees, her pussy presenting to the wall behind her.

I lick my lips and look at Shaw, who is as naked as I am. "Front or back?"

He moves behind her with a smirk, smacking her ass before kneading the cheeks. Her eyes shutter closed briefly before they focus on me as her tongue drags along her bottom lip. My heart skips a beat because she's so fucking beautiful. So beautiful, and all ours.

"Thirsty for my cock?" I ask.

Shaw thrusts into her and she cries out. Her fingers twist into the sheets and her mouth is wide open as he does a few short strokes to stretch her. I smirk, watching her struggle to take his monster of a cock. It never gets old, knowing how tight her sweet pussy is.

I press my tip into her mouth at the next jerk of her body forward when Shaw thrusts. Her soft lips part, sucking me in gently. Moving closer, I hold the base of my cock for her as we use her like our perfect little fuck toy.

On a deep stroke, she moans and the vibrations of her throat have my eyes rolling back. Her drool slobbers all over my cock the longer we go, but she doesn't complain.

Shaw pulls out and flips her onto her back gently. We both move closer, stroking our cocks faster as Mikayla palms her tits. She kneads her generous mounds, twisting her pointy tips.

"I'm sorry I've been a bad girl. Please give me your cum," she whimpers.

Her words hit me right in my balls. "Oh, Jesus. *Fuck*," I cry out as my cock throbs, shooting out ropes and ropes of white jizz all over her swollen belly. Milking my shaft for as much as I can, I finally fall back onto my heels.

Mikayla reaches down, smearing my mess all over her taut skin. Shaw's breathing becomes erratic as he watches her, his stroke uneven as he picks up his pace.

"Beg for Daddy's cum, too," I tell her, smirking when Shaw groans.

She brings her fingers to her lips, licking them clean. "Please, *Daddy*. Paint my skin like I'm your own little whore."

A twisted expression shatters across his face as if his pleasure is painful as his breath stalls. Cum sputters out of his cock, splattering all over Mikayla's chest and the beginning curve of her belly.

I climb off the bed and grab some wet towels, handing them to Shaw. He always enjoys cleaning her up in the moments after we have our way with her.

Grabbing my clothes, I slowly pull them on as I watch him take care of Mikayla. Our family is unconventional, but I wouldn't trade it for anything.

Mikayla

"Are you excited, Mama?" Nurse Jackie beams. "How about you, Grandpa?" She glances at Shaw, her cheeks tinting with blush.

Shaw laughs. "We're so excited. I had to basically fight Gage to be here instead."

Jackie giggles and hands me the cup to collect the urine sample. She barely glances at me as she does, her eyes still bright as they're focused on Shaw. Jealousy burns in me and I glare between the two. Shaw smirks as he catches the look, and I huff, tossing my hair over my shoulder and going to the bathroom.

I know I'm being ridiculous and that I technically have no right to even assert some claim over him. I'm more with Gage than him, even if he likes to fuck me in the middle of the night while I'm sleeping. Once I relieve some of the pressure on my bladder and write my name on the cup, I wash up and go back into the room in a lighter mood. Jackie can flirt all she wants. My daddy is hot, but he's mine.

She pats the chair when she sees me. "Let's find out what we're having, Mama."

I smile, adjusting my leggings lower on my hips. Laying down, I lift my shirt and look at Shaw. His eyes roam over my swollen belly with unmasked heat, making me horny. His tongue peeks out between his lips before he leans back in the chair, opening his legs wider. I smirk, knowing he's hard.

Flinching when Jackie applies the gel to my stomach, I glance at the monitor on the wall in front of me as she pulls out the doppler.

"Alrighty, let's see if Baby wants to cooperate today."

All of us watch the monitor as she moves the doppler around on my belly. She clicks around on the keyboard in front of her, commenting on how the baby is measuring well and within normal range.

"Jesus," Shaw says.

I glance at him, smiling at his awestruck face. "It's crazy, huh? Seeing them makes it so real."

He swallows, nodding.

Jackie laughs. "Men don't get the fun part of feeling the little bugger moving around, stretching out that belly, and trying hard to crack those ribs."

"Ha, no," I agree, having to hold back my hand from rubbing my stomach. "They haven't gotten that bad yet."

"There we go! Good baby, flashing us and making it easy."

Shaw makes a choked noise and I snicker.

Jackie puts the doppler back and hands me some towels. "You want me to tell you? Or just print it out."

"Print it out," Shaw says, and my eyebrows crease in confusion. He winks and I frown again.

She puts the ultrasound photos in an envelope, and Shaw snatches them before I have a chance. I narrow my eyes. If he thinks he can find out what I'm having before me, he has another thing coming.

"Anything else?" Shaw asks.

Jackie shakes her head. "Nope, we're all set. I'm sure Diana will call to set up your next appointment. Have a good day, Mama."

He holds his hand out for me to grab, and I scoff at him.

"Don't start, Princess. Let's get some food and buy you some new clothes, yeah? Gage said you've been bitching about things not fitting."

I open my mouth to snap that I haven't been bitching but take a deep breath and nod. "And then you'll show me the photos?"

"Of course." He grins, and I don't trust it for a second.

He takes me to the mall thirty minutes away from town. His hand rests on my lower back as we walk till I find a shop with a huge maternity section.

I've reached a point where even the dresses I have are feeling tight as they stretch over my stomach. Shaw stays a few steps behind me as I browse the racks of clothes, torn between more dresses or just grabbing some leggings and large shirts.

"Hello! Can I help you or... your husband find anything?" an associate asks warmly. Her hesitant glance flickers over Shaw.

He chuckles. "She's my daughter."

I frown. I'm strangely hurt at his immediate dismissal of being my husband. I mean we could be if that's what we decided was best, for legal purposes.

"No thanks," I say curtly, unable to control my tone. "Me and my *daddy* are just fine."

The associate blushes and nods, leaving us alone. I push at the clothes harder, scraping the hangers against the metal as I linger on his rejection.

"Mikayla. You okay?"

I give him a saccharine smile, grabbing some random shirts and dresses and walking around him. I can feel his watchful gaze as I continue to shop before he finally grabs my elbow.

"You seem a little angry, Princess."

Shaking my head, I give him all the clothes. "Nope, just being the dutiful daughter and milking my daddy for all he's worth."

He licks his bottom lip slowly, his eyes narrowing before he starts walking me towards the back.

"Dressing room?" he asks the associate. She points, the blush still evident on her face.

Shaw leads me into the room, hanging all the clothes as I watch with crossed arms till he turns to me.

"Alright, what's with the attitude?"

I clench my teeth and then sigh. "You didn't even entertain the idea of being my husband.... It hurt."

His face softens. "Mikayla, you know I want to be with you. But we can't be together *like that* in public."

My throat starts to tingle from the unfamiliar rejection. "What do you mean *like that?*"

He sighs, tugging at his beard. "You and I wouldn't be accepted like you and Gage. It would be better for all our sakes if we kept us"—his hand points between me and him—"behind the safety of closed doors."

I know what he's saying makes sense. And maybe it's the hormones causing it to hurt more than it normally would. With a nod, I move to grab something to try on.

Shaw lingers behind for a second as if to say more before finally leaving me alone in front of the mirror. His legs are spread, arms running across the couch as he watches me undress.

"They could think you're my sugar daddy or something," I tease, trying to let go of my earlier hurt.

A low chuckle rumbles out of him, stopping short when I pull off the t-shirt. It leaves me standing in white lacy panties and a nude bralette. My boobs are getting too big for my bralettes, and I might have to upgrade to real bras soon.

"Fuck, baby. Look at you." His voice is rough, and I turn to face him.

"What?"

He gets off the couch, standing before me as his hand rubs my belly. I realize he probably hasn't seen it entirely bare in months now. His other hand squeezes my ever-expanding waist and moves to the mirror, my back flush against his chest.

"Now I know why Gage has been screwing off lately. You're fucking irresistible. He's a strong man to walk away," he whispers into my ear, kissing the shell of it as his fingers drift to pull at my panties. The other is still sprawled across my swollen stomach. "If it was me, I would never leave your tight cunt. Stay buried overnight."

Licking my lips, I help take off my underwear and breathe out. "You should."

His hand pushes at my thigh, and I open my legs so he can push a finger into my already soaking pussy. "Should what?"

"Keep yourself inside me all night after you've had your fun," I gasp when he adds a second one.

"Hmm. Who told you about that? Gage?"

Pouting at him, I say, "I feel how sore I am the next morning, but you're never there"

He sighs. "I know, baby. Next time, I'll stay all night, and I won't even share with Gage. How does that sound?"

I nod, losing my ability to talk as my chest rises and falls rapidly with his increasing touches. It's getting harder to do anything as my belly grows, including catching my breath.

"You're carrying our boy," he whispers, kissing my hair as his fingers pump in and out of me. "You know how incredibly sexy it is to see you pregnant."

"Shaw," I whisper, hating that he just told me about our son like that.

He clicks his tongue. "Is that what you call me, baby?"

My pussy clenches around his fingers. "No, Grandpa."

He growls in my ear and pulls his fingers out. He kicks at my feet. "Open your legs, hands on the mirror, and bend over so I can see that ass, fucking brat."

I do what he says, keeping my head straight as I watch him. His fingers run along my white panties before he pulls them down and bares me to the cold room. Metal clinks as he undoes his belt and unzips his jeans.

"I'm dying for a taste of your sweet pussy, but we don't have a lot of time, and I need to be inside you."

"Please fuck me." I whimper as he steps up behind me, his huge cock running along my wet folds. He pushes into me, stretching me so deliciously before pausing. His fingers twist into my hair, and he pulls my head back. I gasp.

"You think you're cute calling me grandpa when that very well could be my damn kid?" he asks, his dark eyes staring at mine through the mirror. "Huh? I've come inside this greedy cunt as much as Gage has, haven't I?"

I try to nod, but he keeps my head still as he thrusts forward, forcing me to take a majority of him. I moan, not caring if we're heard.

"You're a fucking slut for your daddy's cock, aren't you?" he rasps while his gaze wanders to where he's disappearing between my legs. I gush at his words, it shouldn't turn me on that he talks to me like that. But just like when Gage taunts me for being his whore, I'm getting wetter.

Shaw thrusts deeper and I cry out, my fingers and toes curling. His cock throbs as I tighten down on him.

"Aren't you? Answer me," he demands.

"Yes!"

He smirks, pulling my hair a little more. "Yes, what?"

"Yes, Daddy," I moan, pushing my ass into him for more.

He groans, letting go of me to slide both hands onto my belly and burying himself fully inside me. "You're a fucking sight."

His fingers knead at the taut skin of my stomach as he starts pumping in and out. I close my eyes, enjoying the feel of him.

"You think you can reach yourself, Princess?" he says, picking up his pace.

I shake my head. I don't care if I get off. "Just come inside me. *Please*," I beg, flicking my eyes to his and smirking. "Then you can taste your little princess' pregnant pussy full of your cum when we get home."

"Fuck," he growls, his cock throbbing as he comes. Each spurt of his seed coats my walls in warmth as he holds himself deep against my cervix. "Who taught you to talk like that?"

I bite my lip. "You and Gage are the only men I've fucked."

He pulls out, reaching down and pulling up my panties. Shaw taps my pussy with a silent command to keep it there. His face is confused as he buttons his pants. "You didn't bleed that night."

I slip my dress back on, and my cheeks blush. "Yeah. I, erm. I got a huge dildo, okay? I broke my hymen a long time ago."

He laughs. "Does Gage know you have that somewhere in the house?"

Shaking my head, I point my finger at him. "No, and you're not going to tell him."

Shaw steps forward, kissing my lips, and then stares down at me. "I'm definitely going to tell him. And you know why, Princess?"

"Why?" My eyes narrow to slits.

"Because I'm going to tell him to use it to train that ass so you can take both of us."

My breath whooshes out of me and my pussy throbs.

He smirks, his gaze roaming over me. "Yeah, you're a filthy girl, aren't you? Look how you're already hot for it."

Huffing, I rub my burning cheeks. "Your monster cock is not going anywhere near my ass."

"We'll see." He says, tapping my ass as he gathers the clothes I didn't have a chance to try on. "Let's go, Princess. I think we've desecrated this place enough for today."

Mikayla

I cross my arms over my chest and rest them on my swollen belly while I glare at the men sitting at the table. Gage and Shaw exchange a look, smirking at each other, and I huff out an annoyed breath.

"Sorry, Princess. You just look so cute when you're all mad," Gage teases, reaching for me.

I swat at his hand. "No touching till the meeting is over."

He salutes me with two fingers. "Yes, ma'am."

Shaw sighs, leaning back into his chair. "Don't play into his antics, Mik. You know the drill."

"Maybe he should act like an adult for two minutes," I say, sticking out my tongue.

Gage bites down on his bottom lip. "Come closer. I'll put that tongue to work." He grabs at the bulge of his jeans and I roll my eyes.

"You've done enough, Romeo." I wave at my belly and then straighten my shoulders. "Speaking of, it's time to set some rules."

Shaw's eyebrows raise. "Rules?"

"Princess, it's cute you think you're the one in charge but—"

"Shut the fuck up and listen," I yell, stomping my foot.

Gage closes his mouth quickly. Shaw looks at him amused, but stays quiet himself.

"Rule number one, both of you are going to start coming home at a decent time. As in the streets lights should just be starting to turn on. No more staying at the clubhouse."

Shaw groans. "I'm not sure—"

I narrow my eyes, my nostrils flare, and he cuts off mid-sentence. My lips curl into a mocking grin. "Good boy."

Gage barks out a laugh before wiping the expression off his face when Shaw glares at him. He holds up his hands in surrender.

Clearing my throat, I hold up two fingers. "Second rule. We start building the nursery this weekend, and every weekend here after is for getting the house baby ready."

They both smile at that, and I know their thoughts have gone to the image of a tiny bundle of joy in their arms.

For a couple of tough tattooed bikers, they really are the biggest teddy bears.

"Three. If either of you miss the birth for whatever reason, we're done. No explanations, no second chances. You're stuck in traffic? You better develop the power to teleport."

Gage looks at me incredulously. "Mikayla—"

"Become a vampire and turn into a bat. I don't give a fuck," I continue.

Shaw chuckles, shaking his head. "You got it, babygirl. Anything else?"

"I want a baby shower, but not at the clubhouse," I say with a pout.

Gage sighs. "That's already in the works. And we're having it here."

I look between them, biting down on my lip as my eyes start to water. They both hurry to stand. "I really just don't want to be alone anymore. I want to spend more time with both of you."

Gage grabs me first, pulling me into his arms and stroking the back of my head. I can feel Shaw's hand on my waist as they slide forward to grasp at my belly.

"Don't cry, Princess. We're sorry," Gage whispers into my ear.

I hiccup, burrowing further into his hold as the baby kicks at Shaw's hands. They both freeze and I chuckle.

"Apparently peanut is mad at you too," I tease.

Shaw rubs hesitantly, waiting for another kick that doesn't come. "That was the baby?" he asks.

I nod, blinking up at him as Gage wipes my tears with his thumbs. "He's been really active lately."

"We'll start staying here permanently and let you know ahead of time of any events. How does that sound," Gage says.

"Events I can go to?" I ask.

Gage's eyebrows knit together. "A lot of them can get pretty heavy with the drinking."

When my eyes start to narrow again, he chuckles. "How about the ones that involve the families?"

I shrug. "I guess that's fair."

Shaw smirks. "What else can we do for you, Princess?"

"A bath sounds nice. And a massage."

"You wet, naked, and with my hands all over you. Sounds like the perfect night," Gage says with a smile.

Mikayla

"Mikayla, I love you, but I swear to god if you make me move this again." Gage snarls at me.

I flip him off. "You'll do whatever I say till it's fucking right. Look what your son is doing to me! I can't even see my feet!" I scream back, pointing at my stretched stomach.

I'm 6 weeks away from birth and can barely walk out of the room without losing my breath. Gage's eyes roam over my form before he shakes his head with a sigh. "Go sit down and point to where you want the damn crib."

Sniffling, I rub my belly. "No, sitting is uncomfortable too. It pushes him into my ribs. And I want it over there."

I motion to the wall across from the closest, and Gage's face turns red.

"Are you fucking kidding me? That's where we had it the first time!"

Scowling, I go back to folding all the washed clothes we bought earlier. "And? I wanted to be sure it was the right spot before committing to it."

"Woman," he growls, sending a shot of arousal straight to my pussy. Everything to do with Gage and Shaw makes me this way. I swear they can breathe in my direction and I'll be one touch away from an orgasm.

I smirk and taunt back, "Baby Daddy."

Gage's anger fades as I see a different type of heat bleed in. "Sexy Mama."

His eyes drift to my chest with a smirk, and I cup my breasts, knowing exactly what happened. I blush, hating the fact that for the past week, I've been leaking milk every time I get horny.

He steps closer, placing his hands over mine. "That's so fucking hot every time."

Scowling at him, I try to turn away, but he keeps me in place. "It's not, it makes me feel like a cow."

"Want me to milk these teets, Mama?" His fingers pinch at my nipples.

My neck flushes and I smack his chest. "That's not funny!"

He laughs, pushing down the dress and cupping my breasts. "I'm not joking."

Gage dips down, pulling a nipple into his mouth and sucking hard. I cry out; they have been overly sensitive lately. His touch is almost painful, but my pussy gushes from the stimulation.

"That doesn't look like decorating," Shaw rumbles behind us.

Gage pops off my breasts with a smirk. "Our little princess is gushing from two ends. I think she needs to be fucked."

"Gage..." I hiss. His teeth scrape down my hard nipple, and milk sprays all over his lips. My eyes widen in embarrassment.

Shaw steps next to us. "Jesus, I didn't know she was leaking like that."

"Recent," Gage mumbles. His gaze turns feral as he stands back and grips my dress, ripping it straight down. He lets it go, and it pools around my feet in shreds.

My mouth barely opens in shock before Shaw's chest presses into me from behind, his hands rubbing my belly. His mouth brushes against my ear. "Feed your brother from your milky tits while your daddy plays with your pussy."

I close my eyes as Gage's mouth latches onto one of my nipples again, his fingers playing with the other. Shaw's hand dips between my legs, tapping them to open further. I try, but struggle a bit to shift them open.

"I don't think our princess can handle us in this position," Shaw teases. He starts to push me towards the side.

"No! Not in the rocking chair. Actually, not in this room at all." I grimace, uncomfortable with how far we've already gotten.

Shaw chuckles, lifting me into his arms and carrying me across the hallway to the master suite I've recently started occupying with Gage. He sits on the foot of the bed, and I face them, watching as they quickly strip off their clothes. Shaw cups my face and kisses me attentively, his tongue swiping at my lips before he climbs onto the mattress.

He taps his thighs. "Come here, Princess."

Gage chuckles and smacks my ass as I crawl toward Shaw. I straddle his hips as his hands roam over my protruding belly. His thick hard cock is pressed against his stomach, my wet pussy resting on it. My fingers caress the soft steel shaft, smiling when he twitches from my touch.

"Put me inside you, baby. Ride Daddy's cock."

Palming his erection, I notch him at my entrance and sink down onto him, panting at the stretch. He groans, his fingers caressing my belly as I continue down till my thighs meet his pelvis.

"God, you take me so well now," Shaw praises. Gage moves onto the bed next to me, his hand stroking his cock, and I reach over to pump him myself.

"Milk her tits, get your cock nice and slick to slip into her ass," Shaw says.

"What?!" I exclaim, trying to move away but Shaw keeps me in place.

Gage groans, and I gasp when he pinches my nipple, cupping his hand so leaking drops start to pool in his palm. He brings it to his cock, lubing the hard shaft with my breastmilk.

"Oh my god..." My pussy clenches as I watch him, and Shaw throbs inside me. Gage does it a few more times before moving behind me, and I exhale slowly.

They've fucked my ass a few times over the last couple months, but always separate. I've never taken them both like this.

"Lean forward as much as you can without putting a lot of pressure on the goods," Shaw instructs me, and I lightly press my belly to his.

I jerk when I feel Gage's rigid head poking between my cheeks. I hear him spit, and then I feel the wetness spread against my hole. He slips a finger in and I clench in response, already feeling fuller than ever.

Shaw watches my face as Gage works a second finger in, slowly pumping in and out. Then he pulls out, and the burn of the stretch from his cock working its way inside my ass starts. I squeeze my eyes shut as I hiss out a cry.

"Too much?" Shaw asks, and Gage pauses.

I shake my head. "No, no. Keep going."

Gage pushes forward, making it past the small ring of resistance before he starts to slide in more easily.

"*Fuuucckkkk,*" Gage grunts. "I can feel you. She's so fucking tight."

Opening my eyes, I stare down at Shaw's face, twisted in pleasure. I struggle to breathe, I'm being stretched so full.

"You good, Princess?" Gage asks, his hoarse voice causing me to clamp down on Shaw again.

I nod, my nails digging into Shaw's chest as I struggle to stay up.

"Move, please," I plead, and Gage starts to pump in and out. I moan as he fucks me. Shaw stays still under me for a few moments before slowly starting to thrust up every time Gage pulls halfway out. Neither of them fully extract themselves from where they're buried.

My release builds so fast, I don't even have time to warn them before I'm screaming as I tumble over the edge. Waves of ecstasy wash through me, and I even try to move my hips to fuck them back. I know I tighten so much that I trigger their orgasms.

Shaw comes first, stilling as he pumps deep inside of me, spraying my walls with his hot cum.

"Jesus, fuck," Gage sputters before I feel his own pulsing as he comes in my ass. The same warmth burns within me.

"Oh my god, oh my god," I chant, my eyes rolling back as I feel myself being filled to the brim in both holes with their seed. I pant as their cocks throb till they've drained every drop. Gage pulls out and collapses to the side.

"Shit," Shaw curses and lifts me off his cock as Gage's cum starts to leak between my cheeks. He sets me down on my side and places a pillow under my belly.

Gage cuddles into me from behind, kissing my ear as his hands cups my pussy to catch our mess from wetting the bed. "Someone is a little afraid of cum, as if I didn't feel his dick moving inside you."

I laugh as Shaw scowls at us. "There's still something separating us, I ain't your cum rag to be dripped on."

We laugh harder as Shaw rolls out of bed and walks over to the restroom, grabbing stuff to clean us.

SHAW

Mikayla looks radiant as she rubs at her swollen stomach, surrounded by the men and women of the club. The other old ladies have transformed the entire backyard for their baby shower.

I look over at my son, watching over Mikayla with a smile of his own. To the club and the public, she is his and only his. No one knows what we get up to in our own home. Today is one of those days I wish I could walk over and kiss her on the lips. But it's better if everyone assumes that she is only with Gage.

Sipping the beer, I turn away and walk inside to snack on some of the food scattered on the counter.

"Prez, can I have a second?" Dodge follows after me into the house.

I nod, grabbing some of the tasty little pickles off the plate as I stare at him.

He shifts, tugging at his cut. "I wanted to apologize for Jack."

"Why?" I ask. "You're not responsible for his actions."

Dodge nods, but his jaw tics. "Still, I'm the one who brought him in. He stole from the club, my brothers, *my family*."

"And he paid for it, did he not?" I raise an eyebrow and then pat his shoulder. "No apologies, Dodge. I'm just glad we handled a piece of shit like that, and I'm not talking about the money."

He sighs. "Yeah, that was a shock. I wasn't expectin' that."

I grunt, grabbing some more food. When he doesn't say anything else but continues to stand there, I turn back to him. "What? Got more to say?"

Dodge smirks. "Just congrats, I guess."

"Congrats?"

"Yeah, on another son or grandson. Who knows, right?" he jokes, and I step closer. He raises his hands.

"I'm just sayin'. I don't care, but if you want to keep it a secret… I would be careful how you're starin' at her."

I scowl. "What are you talking about?"

Dodge nods to the backyard. "I saw it before we came in. You looked ready to devour her or as if she hung the fuckin' moon. It was obvious."

"Obvious, my ass," I scoff, checking him with my shoulder as I walk around him. "Only obvious to you because you know. Mind your business, dumbass."

Dodge is like a second son to me, having raised him side by side with Gage and Bear. I know he's telling me from a place of love and protection.

He smirks. "Whatever you say, Prez."

"Dad?" Gage calls out, poking his head in through the door. "Mikayla wants you out here for the presents." He looks between Dodge and me with suspicion before heading back to her.

"I'll say one thing," I turn to Dodge, clapping him on the back. "I'm glad we got all that handled before Mikayla gives birth. That's all that matters to me."

I move to stand next to Bear, who is off to the side from where everyone is gathered but watching.

He glances at me. "Can you believe it? Our kids are having kids. Makes me feel old as fuck, but god damn, do I love seeing that little girl smile at me and call me papa."

Shaking my head, I smile at him. "We are old as fuck. And it kind of makes me proud, you know?"

Dodge's booming laugh can be heard as the little girl in his arms wipes the frosting from her cupcake onto his nose. My heart warms at the sight, and I turn my attention to Mikayla. She's dabbing tears from her face at Lacy's custom blanket, and my chest aches at the entire family we've created.

"Proud?" Bear grunts, sipping his beer.

I nod back towards Dodge. "Look at the father he is. We could barely get them bathed or fed at that age, but he makes it look easy. I'm not taking all the credit, but we sure did the best we could to give them this life."

Bear clears his throat, his loving gaze watching his son and granddaughter. "Yeah. I'd never wish what we went through for them, but I'm happy as hell they have a whole club of people to help support them."

Knocking my shoulder against his, I give him another smile. "Forever, brother."

I look back at Mikayla, catching Gage's suspicious eye. Refusing to acknowledge it, I take a sip and avoid his gaze. The conversation I need to have with them can wait for another day.

Viper comes running around the side, beelining it to me as Gage watches with a stern expression. "Pigs, incoming. Five minutes out."

Bear curses, pulling out his phone as I set my beer down. My jaw clenches and I glance back at Gage. I never asked him about the night he took care of Jack, but I'm positive that's what this little visit is about. Giving him a nod to head towards the house, he whispers something in Mikayla's ear before he follows me into the front lawn.

"There's no way it's about him," my son hisses under his breath as two squad cars pull up and block our driveway full of bikes.

I don't reply as I step forward, pulling at my cut as I feel Bear move to stand behind me. I know if I glanced behind me, Viper will have stood up as Gage's second.

The sheriff climbs out of his car, smirking as he stares at us waiting on the lawn.

"Got yourself a little party going, Shaw?" he asks.

I grind my teeth for a second, then relax my jaw, pasting on a smile. "My daughter's baby shower."

The sheriff glances at Gage, his lips thinning as if to hold back a comment on who the father is of her baby. It has my irritation rising and I step closer.

"How can I help you, Sheriff?" I ask him and his partner, who is still waiting hesitantly by the cruiser.

"We're looking into a missing persons case," the sheriff says with a sniff. He tugs at the belt on his side as he rests hand on one hip. "Jack Bellfield? We haven't seen him around town lately. Have you?"

I cross my arms, staring blankly at the officer in front of me. "Nah. We revoked his cut and sent him packing."

The sheriff stands tall. "Revoked his cut?"

"The dumb fucker was stealing from us so we threw him out on his ass," Bear grumbles beside me.

Looking between us, his eyes narrow as if waiting for more information before he sniffs and looks away. "Well, if you have any information. You'll let us know?"

"Probably not. I told the motherfucker to never come back." I sneer.

He drops his head, shaking it a little and rubs a hand down his face. "Alright."

"Who filed the report? We ain't know anyone worried about him!" Gage shouts as he walks up to my side.

The sheriff looks at my son sharply and it has me moving closer to Gage with a puffed out chest. Gage snorts.

"Some big wig from the city. Put up a large amount too," he finally says with a shrug. With one final nod, he retreats back to his cruiser and leaves.

I blow out a long breath and my shoulders slump as the car disappears down the road.

"Ya think it's trouble?" Dodge asks.

Gage and I exchange a glance, slightly worried it could be.

"I'll have Cowen look into it," Gage says, his jaw tight. "Either way, they ain't ever finding him."

GAGE

Leaning on the bar counter, I watch the prospects carry the kegs outside to the clubhouse truck. Something about one of the clubwhores graduating a nursing program or something. All I know is that Lacy tells us where to go and pick up whatever she needs for the parties.

"Want me to wrap up some bags of ice too?"

I nod at the manager and whistle for Fox to come to me. I've grown fond of the prospect. I'll probably petition the council to patch him soon.

"He's gonna make us some ice. Stack them with—"

A loud commotion on the other side of the bar interrupts me. A drunk man stumbles out of his chair and wipes the spilled liquor down his shirt. The woman that had been parked on his lap starts sobbing from where she's sprawled on the floor after being dumped.

"She's eighteen. You fucking cocksucker!" another shouts.

My eyebrows raise when I recognize the woman as Mikayla's old bestie and the shouting man as the one who she'd clung to when they sneered at my baby mama. The manager standing next to me sucks in a breath.

I chuckle. "She have a good fake or she flashing our bouncers?"

"I'll have to double check, sir."

Shrugging, I turn back to the scene. Even if we do get fined for serving someone under age, they ain't gonna shut us down. We bring in too much money for the city, so they'll look the other way as long as trouble doesn't find us.

"Sean, stop!" Talia cries, pulling at his arm. "We weren't doing anything!"

Sean shrugs her off. "Your tongue was down his throat. You begged me to take off work to hang out with you, and here you are being a slut."

Fox snickers next to me. "I can't tell who is more desperate, him or her."

The grin on my face widens. "Five hundred bucks and I'll get you patched in this weekend if you go over and claim she needs to get checked for chlamydia after sleeping with you."

He winces. "Man, I ain't ever stick it in without a wrap. What if it gets around town?"

"I'll do it!" another prospect pipes up.

I glare at him. "Nah, this is for Fox and Fox only. And it's curable, just say you took your course of meds. The five c-notes should cover it."

His shoulders slump. "Fuck, I'm gonna have to do it, aren't I?"

Dodge laughs. He already knows that if we really like you, you don't get patched in without some kind of hazing.

"Her name is Talia," I offer.

Fox cracks his neck, and storms over. He pushes Sean to the side and moves in front of Talia. Her eyes widen taking in the handsome biker.

"Talia, baby. I'm so happy I found you," Fox says frantically. He pulls at his cut, glancing at the men around him as the tips of his ears turn red. "I have some bad news. I tested positive for the clap, and I lost your number. I wanted to make sure you got tested too after our time together."

Her mouth slacks, floundering open and closed like a fish. "Uhh—"

"Are you fucking kidding me?!" Sean screeches. His wail is so loud and pathetic that Dodge and I instantly burst into side-pinching laughter.

Fox grimaces and slaps him on the shoulder. "Sorry, man."

Then he hurries back to us and I turn my back to the scene, facing the bartender as I try to control myself. "Give the man a beer after that," I say through snickers.

"Cowen's going to be so upset he missed this." Dodge guffaws.

I shake my head. "He'll pull the security cameras for everyone to see."

Fox's face pales. "Cameras?! With audio?"

That sends us back into roars of laughter as the bartender fails to hide his smile, setting our drinks in front of us.

· ♥ · ♥ · ♥ · ♥ · ♥ ·

I line up the shot and smirk at Cowen, bringing the stick forward without tearing my eyes from his. The clank of the ball falling into the pocket has me standing straighter. "Still think I'm out of practice, asshole?"

Cowen flips me off, grabbing the balls from the pockets to rack them. I hand my pool stick over to Dodge as I sit to the side.

Dodge chuckles, patting Cowen on the back as he waits for the man. "Just because he's not here every weekend anymore doesn't mean Gage can't kick your ass."

I raise my beer and salute. "Amen, brother."

"Your old lady already got you on a tight leash and it's only been a few months." Cowen rolls his eyes, polishing his stick with some chalk.

"The only thing tight about my old lady are her fucking pussy and ass. Who knew pregnancy makes women even more horny?" I laugh. But also, if Mikayla wanted me to spend every minute with her, I would. No questions. I love my brothers, but she's my life.

Dodge groans. "I swear my dick got road rash from how much Ember was riding it when she was carrying our baby girl."

"No shit, that's a thing?" Cowen asks, glancing over to a few of the clubwhores at the bar.

Snickering, I finish my beer and shake my head. "Bro, did you not learn a thing from Dodge."

"You're right. That was an insane thought." Cowen grimaces, pressing a hand over his balls.

Dodge booms out a laugh. "Ember might have turned out to be a shit mom, but she gave me my baby girl. I don't regret nothin'."

I roll my eyes. "You know what he was telling me the other day? The club women are only good for one thing."

Cowen's eyebrows raise. "Oh yeah. What's that?"

"That sloppy toppy," I say, trying to contain my laughter.

"That gluck gluck 9000," Cowen adds.

Dodge groans, glancing over at the women. "Fuck, I was drunk. Don't ever repeat that. They'd skin me alive."

"GAGE! Mik says answer your fucking phone!" Lacy shouts across the clubhouse, moving back behind the bar.

I frown, pulling out my phone to multiple missed calls and texts. "Fuck!" I call her back as I'm already heading towards my bike.

"Where the hell are you?" she shouts as soon as she answers. The desperation in her tone sends a shot of unease through me.

"At the clubhouse. I didn't realize my phone was on silent, Princess," I tell her, climbing on my bike and starting it. Dodge and Cowen rush out the door, moving to start their bikes behind me. "What's going on?"

"The baby is coming, obviously! Fuck!"

I nod to Cowen. "Go wake up Shaw. Mik is going into labor!"

Cowen's eyes widen as he shuts off his bike and runs back into the clubhouse. Dodge scrambles to get off his bike and pulls the truck keys out of his pocket. He tosses them to me as we both move to the car instead.

"We're coming with the truck. Five minutes, baby. How many minutes apart?" I put my phone on speaker and hand it to Dodge as we peel out of the parking lot.

"I-I don't know. I can't count them," Mikayla cries. "It hurts." Her hushed confession slashes into me.

"That's okay, we're okay. Remember what the lady taught us? Breathe in through your nose—"

"No! I don't remember anything. Why aren't you here?!"

"Mikayla," I rasp, my chest caving at her defeated tone. My hands tighten on the steering wheel. I shoot through the last intersection before the neighborhood, not caring if it's a red light. Horns blare around us.

"Gage! You getting into an accident won't help her right now," Dodge hisses.

"I'm sorry," she sobs over the phone. "I'm scared, Gage."

"I'm almost there, Princess. Take some breaths for me," I tell her, my throat aching from trying not to succumb to the fears running through my mind.

She's silent as we pull into the driveway. I barely manage to pull it into park and then I'm sprinting to the house. She's leaning over in the kitchen, hands braced on the counter. She moans as I rush upstairs, kicking myself for not moving the hospital bag closer to the door.

Grabbing the duffle bag, I hurry back downstairs, and she's waddling towards me. "Want me to carry you to the car?"

"No," she snaps, rubbing at her stomach. "Don't touch me, just hold me."

My mouth opens and closes, unsure what she wants. Dodge whistles from outside as I open the door, and he holds up the car seat.

"Put it up front for now. I'm getting in the back with her," I tell him as her hand comes to grip my arm with a strength I didn't know she possessed.

I look at her, and the fear swimming through her watery eyes has me pushing my own away. "Bag, check. Car seat, check. Baby mama, check. I think we're good to go."

Mikayla lets out a small laugh. "You would be the one to forget me."

"Probably," I say, walking her to the truck and helping her into the backseat. I climb in after her.

Dodge is backing out as soon as the door closes, grabbing the bag from it and shoving it in the front seat. "How you feeling, Mik?"

"Like something the size of a watermelon is trying to tear through my vagina." Her eyes squeeze shut as her nails break the skin of my arm.

Dodge grimaces. "Shaw texted and said he's heading to the hospital."

Mikayla breathes out loudly. "Good, good. That's good."

SHAW

Mikayla's eyes shine with uncontained happiness as she watches Gage hold the small baby. Gage's face is wet with tears as he rocks softly from side to side with the bundle in his arms. The hospital had a limit of only one person in the delivery room with her. I was upset at first, but after a while, I realized I couldn't take this moment away from either of them.

Her gaze locks to mine, and her smile deepens. "Hi, Daddy."

"Hi, Princess," I say, stepping around the bed to kiss her temple.

Gage's hands tighten slightly on the blankets before he nods to me. "Hey, Old Man. Want to hold him?"

Swallowing down the emotion, I shake my head and sit on the edge next to Mikayla. "Maybe later. Have your moment with your son."

Mikayla frowns, her small hand reaching out to hold mine. "We don't know... who is—"

I bring her knuckles to my lips and kiss them. "He's not mine, sweetheart. I entertained the idea for a bit, but I got confirmation from my doctor. My vasectomy hasn't failed at all. I'm shooting blanks."

Her mouth opens and she glances at Gage before turning back to me. "We were never going to test to find out. It's *our* son."

Shrugging, I smile at her and then Gage. "I've raised a kid already. Two actually. I think it's time to step back."

I clear my throat and get off the bed. Mikayla tries to reach for me but winces and presses a hand to her stomach. I push her to lie down. "Stay, sweetie."

"No. You're freaking me out. It feels like you're saying goodbye." Tears stream down her face.

"It does," Gage agrees, moving to set the sleeping infant into the small plastic crib to the side. "What are you saying?"

"I'm not saying goodbye, I would never leave. But I think I need to step back." I give them a half-smile. "It's always been you two. I'm just trying to slot myself in where I shouldn't."

Mikayla lets out a choked sob. "I don't understand. I thought you wanted to be with me."

Gage's eyes sharpen as he sees how upset she is, turning to me with a hard glare. "Is this really the appropriate time to do this?"

My chest caves in. "You're right. God, I'm sorry. Fuck." I rub a hand down my jaw.

"How long have you felt like this?" Mikayla asks, wiping at her face.

Gage folds his arms across his chest. "Since before the baby shower, huh? I knew something was up with you."

"We can talk about this when you guys get home from the hospital."

Mikayla shakes her head. "Please, I'll just worry about it the entire time. Plus, we're just waiting around at this point."

I sit on the edge of her bed, grabbing at her hand. "I never meant to hurt you, baby. I just think you and Gage are good together, and I don't want to screw it up."

Gage scoffs, moving closer to Mikayla's side. "I didn't take you for an insecure coward."

I tense. "Say that again."

"Gage…" Mikayla whispers.

"Nah. Listen, Old Man. Neither of us has said or done anything to make you feel like we don't want you here. And honestly, I would prefer you with Mikayla than one of those greedy bitches at the club. Love those girls, but they are so desperate for a man it's sickening."

Mikayla pales. "But if that's what you want. If you want to be with them instead of… if that's what you want."

I shake my head. "No, Princess. That's not what I want."

"Then I don't understand."

Sighing, I flick my gaze between them. "How's this going to work, huh? The club may have allowed me to be with her for the initiation, but I doubt they'll be ok with anything past that. What will the town think?"

"Fuck the town, and frankly, fuck the club if they try to shame you. We've done everything for them," Gage seethes.

"It's not that simple. We have multiple businesses here. We rely on their respect for their business."

Mikayla squeezes my hand. "If you're worried about our image, then stay with us. It will look like you're helping with the baby to the outside world."

Gage sighs. "She's right. You were ready to just walk away entirely. What would it matter if you were only with her behind closed doors."

I know they're trying to comfort me and it warms my heart that they still want me to be with them. I glance at the sleeping baby, my chest filling with love and wanting to be a part of his daily life.

"You're really busy anyway. I would rather have a home you feel comfortable in and where you know you're welcome. Plus, I would rather you come to me the nights you're looking for relief," she blushes, tilting to face Gage.

He smiles down at her. "We know you enjoy the mornings you wake up full of cum, Princess. Your greedy pussy begs for it even when you're asleep."

"Shhh!" she snaps. "I don't want the nurses to hear you."

Laughing, I stand and walk over to watch my grandson sleep. "He's perfect."

"You know, you're the only one with experience with the newborn thing. We could use the help," Gage says, bumping into my shoulder.

I roam over my son's face, looking for any resentment. "And the minute you two want privacy, you'll tell me?"

Gage holds up his hand as Mikayla begins to say something. "The minute I want you out, I'll tell you, Old Man."

Epilogue

Mikayla

With a gasp, I sit up and blink at the clock. I scramble out of bed when I realize it's been over six hours since I checked on the baby, and the monitor has been turned off. I run down the hallway and come to a stop at the doorway.

Dillion is sprawled out on Shaw's chest, both of them sleeping in the rocking chair. Shaw's hand keeps Dillion plastered to his bare chest. My shoulders slump in relief, and I shake my head at the adrenaline slowly leaving my body.

I smile at them, wishing I had my phone to take a picture. It's been two weeks since Shaw moved in full-time, clearing out his room at the clubhouse. It's been an adjustment to not wake up in the middle of the night since Shaw's night owl tendencies have been allowing Gage and me some extra sleep.

Frowning, I realize that I had been alone in bed and wonder where Gage has snuck off to. As I walk downstairs, I groan at the sweet smell of coffee drifting from the kitchen.

He smiles at me as I walk up and wrap my arms around his waist. "Good morning, Princess. I didn't expect you to get up so early."

"Coffee, please."

Gage hands me his cup but pulls it away when I try to grab it. I pout at him.

"Remember that thing I wanted to try?"

"No?" I frown, confused.

Gage smirks. "You said I wasn't allowed to use what you pumped and put in the fridge."

My mouth falls open. "Are you really holding the coffee hostage unless I allow you to use my breast milk as a creamer?"

"Yes," he says, his expression serious.

I narrow my eyes. "The answer is the same. The milk in the fridge is for Dillion."

He nods at my chest. "Lemme grab it fresh then."

"Gage... are you serious?"

His hand comes up and pinches at my hard nipple through the shirt, causing a few drops to leak. "Don't you want to feed me too?" His bottom lip pushes out in a pout.

"You have the weirdest obsession with my milk," I say breathlessly as I pull my shirt off, cupping my heavy breast. If I'm honest, I love Gage's obsession with my tits. He's always had it since I could remember. I've woken up many mornings with him resting on my chest, sucking on them as he scrolls on his phone.

When he reaches out to grab them again, I step back. "Remember what I asked for two days ago?"

His face twists. "It's too soon."

"No, my doctor cleared me," I tell him with a shake of my head.

"Cleared you to have sex, but advised you to give your body time to heal before getting pregnant again."

I smile, stepping forward and pressing my breasts against the hands curled around his cup.

"Are you saying you don't want to put another baby in me?" I taunt him.

Gage's eyes narrowed to slits. "You know I do, Princess. You're not going to get my cum in that tight little pussy for a few more months, at least."

I pout. "I could always ask Daddy to reverse his little snip job."

"Do it then," Gage counters. "You still won't be getting a baby from either of us any time soon."

He reaches out and plays with my leaking nipple, his heated gaze watching the white drops roll over his fingers.

"I think you severely underestimate the allure of my pussy."

He looks up at me. "Mik, I love you, but I will always put your safety over my needs."

My heart swells at his love, and I lick my lips. "Fine, I won't push. Hurry up and get your milk."

Shaw

Pacing the room, I wipe my sweaty palms down my jeans. Gage and Mikayla should be returning from dinner soon. We decided to have separate time with her for her birthday this year.

My present to her is a little selfish. It will be for both of us, all of us. The last couple of months at their house living full-time and taking a step back from the club have put a few things in perspective. I want to be with Mikayla, and if I can't publicly claim her, there is something else I can do.

Her laughter echoes up the stairs as they come in the front door. Dillion is at Dodge's, and I know Gage will be going to pick him up soon. I wait at the top of the railing as they make their way in.

Gage's eyes catch mine, and he nods, turning her to me after a quick kiss. "Night isn't over, Princess."

Her smile is wide, and her eyes are bright with warmth as she hurries up the stairs to me. I catch her when she jumps to me, wrapping her legs around my waist.

"You have a good birthday dinner?"

She kisses me and I can taste the faint vanilla traces of whiskey on her lips. "Soooo good."

I laugh, carrying her to my bedroom. "You're not drunk, are you? I planned to have my wicked way with you."

Giggling, she slowly slides down my body as I set her down. "Not drunk, maybe a little tipsy. I just really love my life right now."

The love for our little family spreads in my chest, and I cup her face. "And I love you, Princess."

Her rosy mouth opens in an 'O' shape, and then she rises on her tiptoes to kiss me before twirling away to sit on the edge of the bed. She tilts her chin up and folds her hands in her lap, resting them on her knee crossed over her leg.

"Okay. I'm ready for my present, Daddy."

I scratch the back of my neck, my cheeks flushing. "It's not exactly something I can hand you."

Mikayla frowns. "What do you mean?"

Clearing my throat, I step close to her. "I got my vasectomy reversed."

She inhales sharply, her eyes glittering with tears. "Don't tease me..."

I hold out my hand to pull her off the bed and she stands. Pushing the straps of her dress off her shoulders, I drift my fingers down the inside of her arm till I reach the side zipper of the dark blue material. Mikayla doesn't say anything as it pools at her feet, baring her sexy white lingerie to me. She steps out of the dress and then kicks off her heels. I would have demanded she keep them on, but I have a better idea for tonight.

Shrugging off my cut with the club's logo and my president patch, I hand it to her. "Take off your bra and put this on."

Mikayla's pupils dilate as she hurries. Her tits bounce as they fall from their restraints, and she slips the leather jacket on. My cock hardens painfully at the sight of her naked chest in my cut, and I unbuckle my jeans to relieve some of the pressure.

"You want another baby?" I ask her.

She swallows, her throat bobbing and her eyes misty. "Yes."

"You want *my* baby?"

"You know I do."

Smirking, I strip the rest of my clothes off and stroke my hard cock. "I hope you don't mind, your birthday present is me coming in that pussy for the rest of the night till you're so full of my seed, there's no way I haven't knocked you up."

Mikayla pushes her panties off, scrambling onto the bed and showing me how wet she already is. I let out a long whistle as her hands squeeze at her breasts, pinching and twisting her leaking nipples. Her hips rise and fall lightly as she plays with herself.

"You and Gage already get started at dinner?" I climb onto the mattress, kneeling between her thighs.

She nods. "He wouldn't let me come. Said I needed to be ready for tonight."

"If we start this tonight, you know Gage will have to keep his little dick away from your fertile hole till we know you're pregnant with my kid."

Her lips purse, clearly unhappy with the statement, before she nods. "Fine, but any kids after this will be a free-for-all."

My heart skips a beat. "We haven't even given you a second one yet, and you're already thinking of more?"

"Always," she purrs. "A day doesn't go by without the thought of you two breeding me."

"Fuck," I grunt out. I grab her thighs, pull her towards me, and thrust my cock into her till I'm buried to the hilt. Both of us release a long moan, it's been weeks since I felt the searing heat of her pussy wrapped around me.

Mikayla lets out a low laugh. "I thought once I pushed Dillion out, I would adjust to your size better. But oh my god."

I lean over, kissing her softly as I wait for her pussy to stop fluttering. Reaching between us, I rub at her clit, and she pulls her face away.

"Don't. I'm so close. I want to come together," she whispers.

I trail down her neck, sucking on one of her hard nipples. When I taste the sweetness of her milk, my cock throbs.

"We have all night," I say, muffled against her skin.

"It's my birthday." She pouts, her hands tangling into my hair and keeping my face smashed against her chest. "And I want to come together."

I pull out of her pussy till my thick crown remains barely inside before thrusting forward. "Your wish is my command, Princess."

Mikayla doesn't get another word out as I rise above her, setting my palms on either side of her head, and start pounding into her. Her chest arches up, and I'm unable to look away from her bouncing tits.

"Touch yourself," I growl, fire already licking up my spine. I knew this first time would be quick after I got confirmation the reversal was successful. Knowing I can plant my baby inside her has had me coming almost instantaneously the past few days.

Her hand rubs at her clit as she cries out, her pussy clamping down on me. My cock pumps in and out of her tight cunt, the greedy thing practically begging me to paint it with my seed.

"Fuck, fuck, fuck," I hiss out as I feel the beginning of her orgasm. "Take it, Princess. Take all my cum." I spill inside her, groaning as my balls draw up to my body, pushing every drop into her pussy. Her pulsing walls milk my cock as I keep coming, feeling each throb of cum flooding her.

I fall into her, keeping us locked together as I turn us on our sides. We stare at each other as our panting calms, and I sweep her hair off her sweaty forehead.

"Happy Birthday, Mikayla."

Printed in Dunstable, United Kingdom